HIS RELUCTANT
LITTLE GIRL

Door County Daddies

HANNAH KANE

Published by Blushing Books
An Imprint of
ABCD Graphics and Design, Inc.
A Virginia Corporation
977 Seminole Trail #233
Charlottesville, VA 22901

His Reluctant Little Girl
Hannah Kane

EBook ISBN: 978-1-63954-457-8
Print ISBN: 978-1-63954-458-5

Chapter 1

THE WEDDING...

Dax Dumont watched his bride, Dyani Deere, approach as he waited for her in the gazebo that was adorned with late summer flowers and twinkling lights at the center of the Oneida Farm grounds, giving it a fairytale look. The vision of his bride brought sudden and unfamiliar tears to his eyes. Once again, Dax found it hard to believe that this remarkable young woman who had burst into his life just a few months ago now held a place in his heart forever, as his wife.

Dyani wore her gleaming, straight, black hair loose so it hung almost to her waist. She wore a delicate but exquisitely beaded headband that had belonged to her grandmother. It sat across her forehead and around her head like a crown. Her grandmother's full length wedding dress was made of simple muslin but had been intricately hand embroidered with Wisconsin wildflowers around the neckline, waist, sleeves and hem. The dress had been altered to fit Dyani perfectly. In her hands, she carried a bouquet of purple, lavender and white asters that grew wild on the farm during the last days of summer.

As she walked up the gazebo steps to where the minister and Dax stood waiting, Dyani flashed him a brilliant smile that emanated from her heart. The smile finally did Dax in and he had to wipe his eyes before reaching out to her.

As she gave him her hand and looked up at him, Dyani was struck with Dax's impossible good looks as she was each time she saw him. He stood now, wearing a suit that must have been custom made for his tall, muscular frame and he smiled at her from his strong-jawed face. Her breath hitched and she stopped for a moment so that Dax had to gently tug her up the last step. As she looked up to meet his face, a tear slipped down her cheek. He wiped it away with his thumb as he said, "I love you, little girl." Then he kissed her on the forehead which drew a collective "Aww" from the guests.

The minister stepped forward then and asked the guests to form a circle around the gazebo and take a moment to ground themselves by relaxing, taking a deep breath and bringing Dax and Dyani to the front of their thoughts. Neither Dax nor Dyani had family at the wedding but there were dozens of good friends gathered at dusk at the end of a perfect September day.

The minister motioned for Annie to come forward and said, "The bride's best friend, Annie, will perform the smudging ceremony. As she lights the sweetgrass and sage, the cleansing smoke will help us to invite strength, energy and love into the hearts of this couple and all who are here today."

Annie lit the end of the bundle of herbs to be used in the ceremony, and as it began to smoke and emit a distinctive aroma that was pleasant and peaceful, she held it and a small bowl up in front of herself—as was the custom of their tribe —as she walked inside the circle of guests, saying, "We call on the spirits of all who care for Dax and Dyani—both here and beyond—to wish them beauty, love and grace as they begin their journey together. May they stay grounded and remember to walk with balance, joy and harmony, all the days of their lives."

Annie had come full circle and stopped to put the still smoking herbs on a small altar near the back of the gazebo and the minister began the short official service that would affirm the vows they had made earlier in the year.

When Dax finally took Dyani in a deep and meaningful kiss, the guests clapped and cheered as they were invited into the Oneida Farm Community Center for a reception.

The couple greeted all guests at the entrance to the reception and thanked each one for sharing their day. Dax stood tall and protectively close to his small bride, who frequently stole glances up at her husband and could not help wondering again how she had come to this happily-ever-after life.

Lukas understood that Annie would be occupied at the start of the reception, receiving guests, checking on the food, directing the photographer and all the other duties she saw as her responsibility. Annie apologetically assured Lukas that, soon, she would join him to enjoy the celebration. He took her arm and pulled her in to kiss her forehead, saying, "Don't be long, baby. It's time for you to have some fun."

He made his way to the bar for a beer and then turned to lean on his elbows and watch his gorgeous girl direct the festivities. An older man who had been sitting a few stools away got up and made his way to Lukas. He held out his hand and said, "Hey. I'm Adam Skenendore. I happen to be related by marriage to both the bride and the girl you've got your eye on there."

The man's smile was genuine and warm, so Lukas took

his hand, smiled, and said, "Nice to meet you. I'm Lukas Mattson."

"I'll be honest with you and tell you that I've heard of you from my daughter Issi, who works here at the farm and will be taking the position assisting Annie, now that Dyani is married," explained Adam.

"That's great. I'm sure Annie will appreciate the help," said Lukas, taking another swig of beer.

"I raised Issi since her mother died, so she needs a female role model. I couldn't think of another woman I would want to serve as an example for Issi than Annie. She's smart, strong, compassionate and incredibly hard working. She's so competent that everyone around her relies on her—too much maybe. The only fault I can find with her is that her fearlessness puts her in risky situations sometimes," Adam said thoughtfully.

Lukas had only been listening casually as he kept his eyes on Annie gracefully moving around the room keeping everything running smoothly. Adam's words had Lukas putting his beer down, standing up straight and facing him. His expression became serious—very serious.

"What risky situations?" Lukas asked, trying to speak evenly.

Adam didn't seem to notice Lukas' mood change and continued. "Well, there was that time last winter when a young woman from the tribe was fleeing her abusive boyfriend and found her way to Annie's house in the middle of the night for protection after being beaten. Annie took her in, and as she tended to the girl's cuts and bruises, the boyfriend showed up, angry and drunk. Annie had the presence of mind to call both the tribal police and the sheriff before opening her door and greeting the guy with her Glock 19 trained on him. When he heard sirens, he tried to flee on foot but he was apprehended."

"What?" Lukas roared, not caring that many guests had stopped their conversations and were now looking at him. "She threatened him with a gun?" Lukas was nearly apoplectic.

Suddenly, Adam realized that maybe he shouldn't have shared this story with Lukas. As Lukas wildly scanned the large room for Annie, Adam tried to placate him by saying, "She didn't shoot him, Lukas—just scared him. But Annie is good with a gun. She's won a few marksmanship competitions, you know."

"No, I didn't know," Lukas said, almost in shock at what Adam had to say about Annie. "What happened then?" he asked, nearly choking.

"Annie talked the young woman into pressing charges, so the guy was arrested. Annie let the young woman live with her until she could make a go of it," Adam said with some pride. "She's one of a kind, that girl."

Lukas looked over at Annie, imagining the scenario he'd just heard about, and felt ready to explode. But he knew now was not the time to confront Annie with this information. He had to get outside to calm down. Adam was still talking when Lukas turned to stalk toward the back door of the community center. He needed some air—and space.

Lukas had felt his possessive and protective tendencies becoming stronger and stronger where Annie was concerned, but now he felt out of control. Knowing he would have to wait to talk seriously with her, Lukas headed for his truck to dig out a pack of cigarettes. He grabbed one, lit it and took a long drag. He had stopped smoking about a year ago but still found that a smoke could help him keep calm when necessary. After a second drag, he wandered out to the gazebo where the ceremony had taken place. It was a still, cool night and the sky was clear and star-filled. Lukas took a deep drag as he looked out over the lit yard that ended several hundred feet away at the edge of the woods. It was a beautiful night and he felt himself wind down enough to think straight.

The plan he had for Annie tonight seemed even more appropriate now. He was going to take her home with him and explain his feelings for her. He planned to stress that he would be involved in all things relating to her health and safety. She would need to know that he would be in charge going forward and that while they would discuss things, there would be consequences for her if she continued to take dangerous or unhealthy chances. He hoped to hell it was not a deal breaker but he needed to be honest with her about who he was and what he needed from her if they were to have any hope of a lasting relationship.

Standing there, Lukas reflected on his feelings for Annie. He was a Dom. There was no question that it was part of his make-up and he couldn't—and didn't want to— change that. He had a need to protect and care for the woman he was with. That tendency was always present, but with Annie, it was intense. Perhaps this came from the situation when they met. Lukas had been instrumental in rescuing Annie from the extremely dangerous position she was in. She had been kidnapped and beaten and it was just luck that his experience and connections with law enforcement allowed him to respond quickly when Dax Dumont called needing help to find his girl Dyani. He had been successful in rescuing both girls but it was a close call. Looking back, he realized that it was love at first sight when he saw Annie that night, and his need to keep her safe roared to the forefront of his psyche.

After months of going the traditionally persuasive route to get her to follow his lead, he decided that after the wedding, he would give in to his nature, take her in hand and hope she would not leave him in the dust. Lukas had planned to get her alone after tonight and explain that she needed to lighten her load for her own physical and mental health. But after hearing Adam's story, he was convinced Annie definitely needed a keeper. She had lessons to learn about risk taking and he wanted to be the man to teach her—if she'd allow it.

Lukas crushed his cigarette under his boot and resolutely made his way back to the reception.

Chapter 2

ENTERING THE COMMUNITY CENTER, Lukas scanned the room and found Annie. He watched her do what she had been doing since this wedding had been planned—taking charge and making sure everything went smoothly, even if she had to do it herself. Except for the solemn moments of the wedding ceremony, Annie Summerhill had not stopped to enjoy any part of the wedding reception she had organized for her best friend.

Annie had been planning and working for weeks. She had helped with invitations, directed the decorating of the community center, supervised the caterers, contracted the DJ, picked up the cake and nearly everything else so that Dyani's wedding day would be meaningful and memorable. Though they worked together on many of the details, Annie had taken responsibility for everything going smoothly on what she hoped was one of the happiest days in her friend's life—and it had indeed been a day to remember.

Dyani and Dax had already been legally married at the Brown County courthouse in June, mostly due to Dax's impatience at formalizing their relationship. Dax wanted Dyani to be his wife right away. He had told her she could have a ceremony with an affirmation of vows and a reception later if that's what she wanted—and she did—so she and Annie began planning right away for a September celebration. The ceremony was held at the Oneida Farm Community Center where both Annie and Dyani worked. It had included several traditional Oneida ceremonies which were especially important to the women and the guests who were mostly friends from the farm and the surrounding tribal lands. Both young women were indigenous and had been raised by grandparents who had been elders in their community. Except for Annie's distant half-brother, neither young woman had any siblings. They had grown up thinking of each other as sisters and, indeed, they were nearly inseparable.

As the strains of Unchained Melody began, the room became quiet and Dax moved to the center of the dance floor to hold his hand out and beckon his bride to join him. At first, she sweetly brought her hand up to her mouth in shyness. When she didn't move, he walked toward her. She tentatively moved toward his outstretched hand until they touched and he drew her possessively into his arms as they began their dance, oblivious to everyone and everything around them. Annie finally stopped flitting around and watched them. Dax and Dyani were so clearly in love and Annie knew she had never seen anything as romantic as her friend and her new husband on this night.

Annie's eyes reflected the hundreds of twinkling lights that had been draped back and forth between the upper beams, making the large room seem magical. The scent of sage and lemongrass that was burned in the smudging ceremony earlier lingered in the air as a reminder of the wishes of peace and balance wedding guests had expressed for the couple. Dyani glowed with such happiness that tears gathered in Annie's eyes.

"You gave them an unforgettable day, Annie. I'm so proud of you—really," said a familiar voice from behind her that was so deep, it vibrated within her. Annie turned and looked up—way up—to see Lukas Mattson, the man who had become her self-appointed protector six months ago when he rescued her from a nightmare. Since then, Lukas had been chipping away at the defensive wall of independence Annie had built around herself after an unsuccessful marriage. Annie fiercely protected herself from being hurt again and felt the need to prove to the world that she could take care of herself. Several men had completely given up on her—but not Lukas. He had been powerfully attracted to Annie the first time he saw her and he'd been willing to work slowly and tenaciously to win her—until tonight. His patience was at an end. No more Mr. Nice Guy.

As she did every time she saw him, Annie nearly gasped at his incredible good looks. Lukas was truly a giant. He was 6'5", with broad shoulders and chest and muscular arms. Though his waist was trim, his long legs were the size of small tree trunks. His shoulder-length, dark-blond hair was pulled back warrior style, as was his preference. His blue eyes usually twinkled with good nature—though Annie had seen them appear thunderous when angered. The beard that graced his strong, angular face was the feature that made him look almost ferocious, but it could not hide the dimple that appeared when he smiled his easy and sure smile. Even before Annie knew he was descended from them, she recognized that Lukas' Swedish heritage made him look like a modern-day Viking.

Annie had known Lukas for about six months and, at first, found his authoritative and stern manner to be old-fashioned at best and caveman-like at worst. It was just the kind of behavior she was trying to avoid in a relationship, but as time passed, she was surprised to find herself feeling safe, protected and cared for by the high-handed giant. When she realized that she even found his manner somewhat arousing, she spent a lot of time and energy trying to talk herself out of it but she could not seem to fight what came naturally. Adding to her dilemma, she would find him doing something incredibly thoughtful, like building the raised gardens she had always wanted next to the center or tenderly snuggling a litter of new barn kittens. He was an enigma for her most days, but tonight, he was simply gorgeous and he took her breath away.

"You look stunning, Annie. Would you do me the honor of dancing with me?"

She didn't argue but let him put his hand in the small of her back and lead her out onto the floor. Then he pulled her in close so she could follow his lead. Annie allowed herself to completely enjoy being held in the arms of her Viking until the song ended and she reluctantly began to pull away.

Lukas gently held her arm, keeping her close.

"I have to go, Lukas. I have to make sure…" she said, still trying to reclaim her arm.

"No, Annie. You don't. You don't have to make sure of anything," he said, directing her off the dance floor.

"But—"

"No buts. You have worked that pretty little ass off all day —and night. Christ, you've been running yourself ragged for weeks. You're done now. You're going to relax, have some champagne and another dance with me," Lukas said in a tone that brooked no argument. "There is nothing that can't wait or that someone else can't do."

Annie looked around the room nervously at first but then turned to him and said, "Maybe you're right. I'm getting pretty tired. I'm just afraid that if I sit, I won't get back up again."

"I can help you, baby. We'll figure everything out later," he said, leading her to a chair at an empty table, grabbing two glasses of champagne on the way.

He could see that she was tired but she was still absolutely gorgeous. Her mass of soft titian hair was pulled up to the top of her head but tendrils spilled down, framing her distinctive face. Annie's cheekbones were high and sculpted, enhancing the almond shape of her nearly black eyes. Her lips were full and inviting and her skin tone reminded him of melted caramels. The blue dress she wore was traditional in that it was made from naturally dyed muslin and was embroidered with flowers, much like Dyani's dress. But Annie's dress allowed her shoulders to be bare. It was also quite short—so short that it made Lukas uncomfortable. Her shapely but athletic legs were enhanced by the three-inch heals that still did not allow her head to reach Lukas' shoulder. He had noticed the looks she had received from every man at the reception and had to tamp down his jealousy.

The evening progressed without a hitch due to Annie's careful planning and, finally, Lukas found himself watching Dyani embrace Annie with tears of gratitude in her eyes as the bride and groom got ready to leave.

Dax had wanted to take Dyani on a two-week honeymoon to Hawaii right away, but Dyani had begged him to postpone it until later in the year. She was nearly ready for her first gallery show of ceramics during Art Fest in October. Art Fest was the last big artist gathering in Door County for the calendar year and her friend Sage had encouraged her to show her work. After the show, Sage would help her launch a website from which her work could be sold. Sage was a creative and successful web page designer for many entities but her favorites were artists. Dyani was her friend, so she had outdone herself with the design and special features of Dyani's site.

All of this was happening in just two weeks and Dax knew how much it meant to his wife. He wanted to show his support for her art and her new venture so he moved the reservations for Hawaii to spring, which would be a welcome trip after a Door County winter. For now, they would spend their wedding weekend up at their vacation home on Washington Island and then come home to get to work.

Lukas knew that because the young women had rarely been apart, this new life for Dyani was bittersweet for Annie. He came up behind her and pulled her back against him in an effort to support her and dispel her sadness. As the truck carrying the happy couple pulled away, Annie watched until it was out of sight and then turned in Lukas' arms, looking up at him with unshed tears. "My sadness is selfish," she said.

"Oh, baby, I know this is hard," he said, kissing her forehead. "You don't have her to yourself anymore. But remember that Dyani doesn't live far away and she'll be down here at the farm on a regular basis. Besides, you can see how she loves him. She's happy. It will be okay."

"I know," she said, standing on her toes to plant a soft kiss on his lips. "Thank you." Lukas noted that this was the first time she had ever initiated a display of affection and he smiled, thinking that his undemanding but steady pursuit of a relationship with her may finally be paying off. Annie prided herself on her independence and Lukas was used to storming in and taking what he wanted. He was willing to be patient with this girl—to a point.

Guests were leaving and things were winding down now as Lukas noted how exhausted Annie looked. He had watched her overwork herself for weeks now as she prepared for the wedding and he had decided to take matters into his own hands. Now was the time for him to put his plan in action. Lukas lifted Annie at the waist to sit her on up the bar.

She squealed and said, "What are you doing? Stop, Lukas, I have lots to do."

Before she could squirm down, he grabbed the shoes off her feet, sure that he heard her moan softly. "You have nothing more to do tonight. They're going to take care of everything that needs doing and even come back tomorrow to finish up if necessary," he said, nodding his head in the direction of s a small group of Oneida Farm staff who waved at her sheepishly. "I'm taking you home, Annie Summerhill. Understand?"

She looked over at the young staffers who were already moving furniture and loading gifts into a storage room and then at Lukas' determined face and said, "I guess I don't have a say in this?"

"Nope. None at all." And with that, he picked her up, walked out the door into the cool night, and settled her into his truck. He covered her in a soft blanket he kept in the cab and Annie immediately relaxed. She must have been truly tired, as she fell asleep before she realized that Lukas was taking her to his home—not hers. He'd deal with that fallout later. Tonight, he wanted to be sure she got some rest.

Chapter 3

ANNIE DIDN'T WAKE, even when Lukas pulled his truck into the spacious garage at his sprawling country home just outside Brussels, in neighboring Door County. The home was way too big for one man, but Lukas had spent an idyllic childhood there, and when his parents died within months of each other just a few years ago, he could not bring himself to sell, so he moved back to his family homestead. The adjoining property was his grandfather's old farm where his best memories lived. It was now leased out to a kind and hardworking family—Swedish, of course—who were happy to see Lukas hiking the woods and occasionally lending a hand.

Lukas' father had been a successful farmer but had also accumulated a fortune in Door County real estate, and when he died and left everything to his only son, Lukas was set for life. He would not have to work but, instead, he used his law degree to do mostly pro bono work in Green Bay along with honing his skills as a private investigator, helping out with Green Bay police, sheriff's department, and most recently, Oneida tribal police. In the last year or so, he had become involved with several cases involving the jurisdictional quagmire between tribal, state and federal law enforcement. He had met Annie when he was called in to help with a dangerous rescue and then a complicated legal mess. Since then, he had cut his caseload in both jobs to make time to volunteer at the Oneida Farm, doing work he truly enjoyed but mostly to keep an eye on and be near the independent-to-a-fault Annie Summerhill.

Annie had kept him at arms' length for months after the rescue while Lukas patiently waited for her to give in to what he believed to be a mutual and strong attraction. He had decided to take matters into his own hands—to use the distraction of the wedding to finally take charge. It was now or never. He looked over at the beauty sleeping in the seat next to him and knew what he wanted.

He unfastened Annie's seat belt and began to carry her into the house when her eyes fluttered open. As she looked around and realized where she was, she tried to extricate herself from his arms.

"Why are we here? You can't do this, Lukas! Take me home now!"

He chuckled as she tried harder to squirm out of his arms and he lifted her through the door into a large back foyer and said, "I *have* taken you home, Annie—my home."

"Put me down," she demanded loudly.

"I'll put you down. Right here," Lukas said as he sat her on the island counter in his kitchen. He removed her wrap and then held her wrists comfortably yet effectively at her sides. She tugged against him unsuccessfully, trying to get loose, but he kept her in place with almost no effort. She was fully awake now and he could see her hackles were up. But he had put up with Annie's stubborn resistance for almost six months, and now he was ready to call her bluff.

"A tantrum won't work, Annie. You're going to listen to

me now or I'll put you over my knee and give you the spanking you've deserved for a long time," he said with authority. "Understand?"

Annie had never seen Lukas like this, and though she was still angry and frustrated, she was also surprised to hear him finally take her to task. She had always been able to get her own way as far as he was concerned, but something was different now and she wasn't sure at all that he wouldn't carry out his threat.

"Okay, okay," she said with attitude.

"Try that again without the sass," he said with a frown.

When she hesitated, he lifted her off the counter and bent her under his arm in one move. Then he swatted her bottom several times until he heard her outrage turn to squeals of pain. He had made sure the swats were hard enough to be felt through her dress. Without righting her, he asked again, "What was that?"

Annie didn't know this version of Lukas, but her bottom was stinging and she was really too tired to argue with him.

"I'll listen, Lukas. I'm sorry. Please let me up," she said, sounding sincere and tired.

He lifted her back up to the counter and noticed with satisfaction that she winced slightly. "And no arguing, either. Hear me out," he said, taking her chin in his hand so she was face-to-face with him.

"Yes, Lukas," she said with a compliance he had never heard from her before and that he rather liked.

"All right," he said as he kissed her forehead. "I decided that it was best for you to come to my house, where I can make sure you rest. I knew that if I didn't get you out of there, you'd stay all night cleaning up from the reception no matter how tired you were. You'd be getting everything ready for the center to be back in business on Monday and then probably find more to do," he said, still holding her hands at her sides. "Do you think I'm probably right on that?"

She looked at him steadily, thinking about disagreeing, but said, "It does sound like what I'd do. But still, you can't just pick me up and—and kidnap me. You are so highhanded!" she huffed.

Lukas put a finger on her lips and said, "Look, Annie, I've watched you work for six months now, and you never give yourself a break. I've talked and talked with you about it and you simply don't listen. So tonight, you'll do things my way. I paid that army of college students you have interning at the farm to take care of everything tonight and tomorrow. You're staying right here," said Lukas, who seemed absolutely immovable on the matter.

"Aargh! Lukas Mattson, you are the most arrogant man I have ever known and—"

"Stop," he said more sternly, "I'm not finished. Here's what's going to happen tonight. You're going to go to sleep in my guest room. If you want to take a shower and eat something before bed, that's fine. I'll make something for you. Also, I have your phone so no one will be able to bother you about anything nor will you be able to check on things that no longer need your attention. I may or may not give you back the phone tomorrow, depending on how you cooperate between then and now."

Annie's jaw dropped open at the announcement that he had taken her phone and it took everything she had not to rail against that action, but she honestly didn't have the energy. She did, however, cross her arms in front of herself and roll her eyes.

Lukas' patience was just about gone. He lifted her down to stand in front of him, put his huge hands on her shoulders and said, "This is fair warning, Annie. If you don't cooperate and do what I ask *without* the eye rolling and attitude, I will turn you over my knee again and those little swats from before will seem like nothing. Are you hearing me?"

Annie's eyes widened while she considered her experience with him. Lukas had been volunteering at the farm a few times a week since they'd met. She had caught wind that both staff and guests talked secretly about how odd it was to see Annie—a little slip of a thing—take on Lukas, a Nordic giant, and get her way every time. He had tried bossing her around many times, but she rarely complied. Tonight, something had changed but it was difficult for her to give up. For a moment, she considered challenging his threat as she narrowed her eyes.

Lukas looked down at her, appearing every bit the Viking warrior. His eyes blazed and his mouth was set in a tight line. There was no sign of the amiable dimple he usually sported but, instead, she saw an unfamiliar tick in his cheek. Annie finally decided this was not the time to be defiant.

Lukas watched her face go from stormy anger to compliant defeat quickly as she said, "I'm sorry, Lukas. Maybe you're right that I have been working too hard lately. And you're certainly right that I'm tired. Please don't be angry with me." Then she stood on tiptoes and kissed the bottom of his chin—the only part of his face she could reach. "And you know, I think I would really like to just go to sleep. Can I shower and eat in the morning? Please?"

That handsome apology took the wind right out of his sails so he sighed and said, "Sure, baby. I really want you to rest. My sister has some clothes, pajamas and things, in the bedroom next to the master. I think you'll find what you need there." Annie peeked down the hall as he turned on hallway lights. "Last room on the right. I'll check on you in a while."

As she looked up at him, he took her face in his hands, kissed her gently on the lips and said, "Be a good girl and go get comfortable." That tender command shot a charge like electricity through her core.

Lukas made himself turn away and leave her there before he took things any further. It had been torture for him to honor the distance she had insisted on maintaining since they met. Annie hung tightly to her image of independence and self-sufficiency. Oneida Farm was a large operation, and though she was young, she was the most senior staff member. Now, he had decided to assert himself and force the issue of her coming away with him to take a break. He hadn't known what to expect but had been pleased with her reaction. Maybe he was making some headway with the stubborn little girl.

Chapter 4

BY THE TIME Lukas locked up and returned to the guest room with a bottle of water for Annie, she had collapsed on the bed, fully dressed, and was asleep. He tried to ignore how her short dress had ridden up her trim, golden thighs and her sexy black lace panties were peeking out. Again, he felt a sense of victory that he had succeeded in bringing her to his home so he could insist she rest, but he decided she would sleep better if she changed into pajamas. He found some kitten-soft sleep pants and a tank top in the dresser where his sister kept some clothes for when she visited and sat down next to Annie on the bed.

"Hey, baby," he said, pushing a curtain of gleaming black hair off her face. "Let's get you comfortable and into these pajamas. Come on. Sit up for a minute," he said, pulling her to sit up.

Without opening her eyes, she batted his hands away and sleepily mumbled, "No. I'm fine. Leave me alone." She flopped back down, trying to ignore him.

He stopped for a moment, looked down at her, and his

breath hitched. She was gorgeous. Her mass of black hair spread wildly across the pillow and quilt, her thick dark lashes resting just above her high cheekbones, and her hands drawn under her face as she attempted to snuggle in like a child made his eyes darken. The dress she wore wasn't too tight but did embrace her curves like a glove and her soft shoulders and legs were bare. His cock began to complain.

Lukas renewed his efforts to undress her quickly and get her into pajamas and he wouldn't be deterred. He'd made a decision that this would be the weekend when he'd set Annie straight and establish his position.

He lifted her toward him so he could unzip her dress and quickly pulled it down to her hips. Her brow furrowed and she pushed against him but her resistance was weak. When he realized she wore no bra, his cock came alive. Even though he moved as fast as he could and tried not to stare, he was able to see that Annie's breasts were generous for such a small woman. Her dusky nipples called out to be suckled and he had to force himself back to the task at hand. Removing her dress completely, he saw that she was naked but for the scrap of a black thong she wore. The sight took his breath away. Lukas grabbed the tank top and struggled to get her into it. Still sleepy but awake enough to resist, she pulled her arm away. Desperate to get her covered, he turned her and administered a swat so solid that she stilled long enough for him to slip the tank top on. Her eyes flew open then as she screeched, "Stop it!" She hit him more forcefully then.

"That's it, Annie," he growled as held her in position and swatted a few more times until she allowed him to get her into the sleep pants.

"Leave me alone, Lukas! Please!" she pleaded.

'Leaving her alone' would be one of the hardest things he had ever done, but he grabbed the quilt and covers out from underneath her, picked her up at her waist, and tossed her gently onto the bed before covering her up. He thrust the bottle of water into her hands and said gruffly, "Drink some of this and go to sleep. Now, Annie."

As she sat up and took a few swigs of water, he noticed tears on her cheeks. He wanted to wipe them away but was afraid to touch her. He handed her a tissue and said more gently, "I'm at the end of the hall if you need me. Sleep tight, little girl."

Christ, Lukas thought. *This girl has me tied up in knots.* He had to get in the shower and take care of himself, thinking he could maybe then relax, but that wasn't enough. He wrapped a towel around himself and went to grab a beer. He stood at the windows that overlooked the woods, drank his beer and tried to put Annie out of his mind. But he was wide awake with visions of that sleepy but luscious body front and center in his brain. As long as she seemed to have seriously permeated his thoughts, he might as well use this time to come up with a plan. He cared about her and wanted to begin a relationship that went deeper than she had allowed so far. Annie Summerhill would be a challenge, but he was up for it.

First, he wanted to date her in the way most people began—going out to eat, attending events, and enjoying quiet times together to come to know each other. They hadn't met under normal circumstances, but rather under some intense ones. Lukas' protective and possessive instincts immediately had taken over and never receded. Though she fought it, Lukas insisted on checking in on her every day for the first couple of weeks after the incident. As Annie managed Oneida Farm near Green Bay, Lukas began stopping there every day after work, much to Annie's frustration. That meant he had to drive from his office in Green Bay to the Oneida Nation and then back up to his home in Brussels,

Door County. The trip took about an hour but he thought it absolutely necessary.

She'd been healing from a wound on her arm where a bullet had grazed her and also from a concussion—both sustained in the kidnapping attempt from which he'd rescued her. Though the healing seemed to be going well, he insisted she go to follow up doctor appointments. When she was released from the doctor's care, he could have ceased stopping in but, by then, he was very attracted to Annie. In fact, she fascinated him. He watched her work hard, making sure everything went smoothly at the farm. She was directly in charge of nearly all aspects of operation there, the community and education center, the gardens, the farmers' market and the museum. Even the men involved with the cattle operation seemed to look to her for some decisions and leadership. She lived in a rented house on tribal lands not far from the farm. When he found out she lived alone, he insisted on installing a security system to keep her safe, though she protested strongly.

The more he visited, the more he wanted the beautiful and capable woman, and though he knew she was also attracted to him, she worked hard not to let anything develop. He had also grown to really enjoy his time volunteering at the farm. It was an incredible place that represented a legacy of Oneida history and community along with a working farm with productive vegetable gardens and a specialized cattle operation. Having been raised on a farm, Lukas was happy to cut his work schedule down so he could volunteer there two full days a week. At first, he used the volunteer work as an excuse to see Annie—to check in on her. And while he was able to accomplish that, he also came to respect the crew of men who worked there. His experience was valuable and he had become a popular and needed volunteer.

From his vantage point, Lukas had observed all that Annie did at the farm and decided it was too much. She actually did the work of two or maybe even three people. Lukas had talked with her many times about her exhausting schedule, to no avail, and when he went over her head to talk to her boss, Annie had not spoken to him for a week.

Lukas' initial and powerful reaction to Annie only grew over time, so that by the time the wedding day arrived, he thought he might be falling in love. He watched her work night and day to assure that Dyani had a memorable day, and while he understood her devotion to her friend, he didn't like her working herself to exhaustion. If she were his, he would not have allowed it, but she wasn't his—yet. He had decided to furtively make a plan that would force her to take some down time as soon as the wedding was over. He knew she probably wouldn't like that, but she would have to deal with it.

Keeping an eye on Annie at the wedding and watching the way Dax and Dyani seemed to love each other so deeply, had motivated Lukas to think that it was now or never. He would make it clear to her that he was the one in charge and she would need to honor his desire to watch over her or pay the consequences—and those consequences would include bare-bottomed spankings.

He believed he could allow her independence while also providing a space for her to sometimes submit to him—to be cared for and supported—and punished if necessary. Lukas was a Dom and knew he would be happiest with a woman who would give over to his Daddy tendencies. While he didn't need his little girl to be a "little"—with childlike dressing or toys—he did want her to submit to the kind of care, safety and discipline a Daddy figure could provide. Lukas was not sure how Annie would eventually respond to this need of his, but he knew he couldn't change who he was.

He hoped Annie would come to appreciate this dynamic and be able to go forward with a serious relationship. If she couldn't accept it, he would have to walk away. It was a real dilemma for Lukas. Sleep evaded him until almost dawn.

Chapter 5

THE WELCOME SMELL of coffee caused Annie to smile even before she opened her eyes. She was nestled down under a soft quilt and silky sheets of a thread count she had never experienced. The comfort was almost decadent. But she was not at home. Lukas had brought her to his home last night without asking her. He claimed that he knew she would not rest appropriately if she stayed home and that he knew she was exhausted. He had become such an enigma. Lukas could be kind and thoughtful and the huge man certainly was beyond handsome, but he was often impossibly high-handed and bossy. Annie was not used to a man like him. Sometimes his bossiness was beyond the pale, and last night, he had taken advantage of her exhaustion.

Annie allowed herself to think about Lukas as she snuggled cozily in the luxurious bed. She had to admit that she had been struck with his searing good looks the first time she saw him. She had never known a man as tall and muscular as Lukas and was a little surprised she found his size so wildly attractive. Around him, she felt small and feminine, which was not something she would have thought appealing. She was independent, self-reliant, and strong. But as she thought about how Lukas had taken her in hand since last night, she could not deny the tingling in her belly—or was that lower? She was shocked and frankly disappointed in herself to find that she was aroused at his dominance. It was a completely new and foreign feeling for her. But it was certainly real.

Annie forced herself back to the moment, and in addition to bacon, she could smell something baking. She had been so busy at the wedding the night before that she had barely eaten, so she was starving. She found the ensuite equipped with everything she needed to clean up and after she scrubbed her face, brushed her teeth and hair and donned a sweatshirt she found in the dresser, she made her way to the kitchen.

Barefoot, she was able to approach the kitchen silently, and as his back was to her as he cooked eggs and bacon, she could watch him unobserved—something she had never done before. My God, he was a giant! She knew this, but now, even in his enormous and high-ceilinged kitchen, he still filled the room. Lukas was wearing a gray t-shirt that stretched tightly over his powerful chest and arms. His jeans fit perfectly over his long, thick legs and an ass so sexy, she could feel moisture gathering in her panties as she took it in. His thick, blond hair was pulled back, making his face appear even more angular and strong than usual. Somehow, the fact that he was barefoot was also sexy as hell. Annie's ire, along with her plan to read him the riot act for "kidnapping" her, dissolved as she melted against the kitchen doorway.

He looked up suddenly. "Well, good morning, sunshine. Are you hungry?" he asked as she watched his dimple appear through his trimmed beard, and she felt what was now becoming a familiar current of arousal.

Feeling like she had been caught in the act, Annie blushed and could only stutter, "Yes, I'm hungry," then, gulping, said, "thank you." Her eyes could not meet his, and as he turned to pour coffee into large mugs, she held her cold hands up to her face in an effort to hide her embarrassment. She had been around him many times but something was definitely different now.

Lukas plated their meals and sat across from her at the breakfast bar. Besides another quiet, "Thank you," Annie said nothing. She had never felt this lack of control and was struggling mightily to tame the butterflies fluttering deep inside her. Struggling with those butterflies while still angry that he had brought her here without consulting her, Annie thought it best not to speak until she could work out her conflicting emotions.

They ate quietly for a while until Annie bit into a warm buttered muffin and made a small moan that caused his breath to catch.

"Mm, this is so yummy," she said, looking up at him as she used the tip of her tongue to gather crumbs off her lush lips. "Thank you, Lukas. Breakfast is wonderful."

"I'm glad you like it," he said, smiling but inwardly groaning at the effect the appearance of her little tongue had on his cock.

Avoiding his look, she began to stand up to take her plate to the sink.

"Sit," he commanded. "I'll clean up."

"But—" she began.

"You have two choices. You can settle in on the sofa in front of the fire and let me bring you another cup of coffee, or you can take a shower," he said, giving her a direct look.

She chafed at this new large-and-in-charge Lukas but decided that this was not worth arguing over and, with a huff, turned to head down the hall, saying, "I'll be in the shower."

"Use the one off my bedroom," he called after her.

Wanting to maintain some autonomy, she didn't turn back but answered over her shoulder, "I'll just use the one in my bedroom."

She had just grabbed some jeans, a light green sweater, and some short boots she thought might fit when, suddenly, Lukas' body filled the doorway. Before she could say anything, he took the clothes from her, gently grabbed one of her arms, and began guiding her toward his bedroom.

"You're going to use this shower," he said as he turned on the lights in the biggest and most well-appointed bathroom she had ever seen. There was a huge, open shower, featuring a large rain head with nozzles and gadgets everywhere. Lukas reached in and activated a sound system that began to play soothing music. Then he turned on the water and smiled down at her. Annie still looked a little stunned that he had succeeded in bullying her so easily.

"Enjoy," he said as he chuckled and closed the door behind himself.

She had never taken such a long and luxurious shower. As the stress of work at the farm and the recent wedding preparations began to fade, she allowed Lukas to fill her thoughts. She realized that she had been attracted to him almost immediately and that she had been fighting that attraction since the moment she met him, months ago. Annie had suffered through a disastrous young marriage and not had many positive experiences with the opposite sex since then. Her husband, Elan, had not been mature enough to settle down, partying with friends nearly every night. When Annie found he had been unfaithful to her—repeatedly—she'd filed for divorce. He had beaten her then and she had needed a restraining order to keep him away. Because Elan was a non-

Native, it was difficult to make the restraining order hold. The tribal police and, indeed, their entire judicial system was understaffed and there was a lot of ever-changing gray area complicating the non-Native and tribal systems. It was unlikely that Elan would ever be convicted of beating her so it worked in her favor when Elan's life took a darker turn then and he ended up in prison for dealing drugs. Her miserable experience with Elan had convinced her to keep her distance from men and throw herself into the work she loved at Oneida Farm.

It was tempting to think that Lukas and she might have a chance but, in reality, Lukas could not be more different than she. He was a highly-educated man, with an advanced law degree. He had also been a detective with the Green Bay Police Department and the Door County Sheriff's Department and had achieved a reputation as one of the best investigators in the area. He was well-spoken, well-traveled. sophisticated and apparently quite wealthy. He came from a stable and successful family. In contrast, Annie was raised by her grandfather as her father had been an alcoholic and her mother had left them both when she was quite young. She had no degree, and though she had a job she loved and was good at it, she believed she brought nothing to the table for a relationship with him. She felt unworthy and, in an attempt to shield her heart, she had used a lot of energy keeping her distance from him, both physically and emotionally, in the six months she had known him. When he insisted on checking on her after the kidnapping incident and then showed up to volunteer regularly at Oneida Farm, she had difficulty avoiding him, and though he had not pressed her for so much as a date, he seemed to be always in her path. He had honored her independence and desire to maintain distance —until last night.

Lukas had suddenly become assertive. While she appreciated that he cared enough to notice she was stressed and tired and then had planned a sort of getaway for her, she struggled with how she felt about the dominant side he had shown her. And she was truly shocked to find that when he spoke sternly, she felt the need to clench her thighs. There was no doubt about that and she couldn't seem to control it. In fact, as she moved her soapy hands over her body under the soothing water, she could not help but wish it was his huge hands caressing her. When she found herself reaching down to pleasure herself, she suddenly decided to get a grip, and quickly rinsed, turned off the shower and stepped out to dry her hair. That was too close for comfort. She made a decision that she would dress and ask him to take her home right away.

Donning the clothes she found and finding that they fit remarkably well, she made her way out to the great room to find him. He wasn't there, nor was he in the kitchen, but then she saw him out on the expansive deck, standing quite still with his powerful arms braced on the railing, looking for all the world like a sea captain from a romance novel. She could see the strong angles of his face in profile as he seemed to be intently watching something she couldn't see. When Annie put her hands up on the glass door, Lukas caught her movement and turned to her, putting one large finger over his lips, signaling her to come out with his other hand. The sight of his god-like body and ruggedly handsome face caused a sudden warmth to shoot all the way through Annie's core and she felt like her insides were melting.

She opened the door carefully and almost silently approached Lukas, whose arm was extended to her. He pulled her close and wordlessly pointed out onto the prairie-like area surrounding his home. There, only about fifty feet away, was a mother deer and her two fawns, peacefully eating from Lukas' vast garden.

He watched as Annie's face lit up with such tenderness and delight that he could see unshed tears in her eyes. She put her hand up to her mouth in wonder. And when she raised her smiling eyes to his, he was sure he had never seen a more beautiful woman anywhere. Later, he would wonder if that was the moment he fell in love. Annie was still watching the deer, but Lukas only had eyes for her. Annie's titian hair shone brightly in the morning sun and her flawless skin begged to be touched. He had pulled her so close that their bodies touched from knee to shoulder. Annie's little body vibrated with need as Lukas became uncomfortably hard. The deer scampered off then and she looked up at him. When Lukas lowered his face to hers to kiss her gently, she didn't pull away, but rather welcomed the soft coupling. He deepened his kiss while his arms tightened around her. Annie stood on tiptoes and reached to put her arms around his neck, trying to match his passion but not quite able to reach—he was so incredibly tall. When she whimpered in frustration, he lifted her with one massive hand under her bottom and encouraged her legs around his waist. Their tongues met as they kissed hungrily, but when Annie emitted a delicious moan, Lukas pulled back. They were quickly reaching a point of no return and his plan had been to take things slowly.

Annie reluctantly lowered her eyes as she seemed to understand his action and she squirmed to get down. However, he didn't let her go but said, "I think we need to talk," as he sat her on the deck railing, stood between her legs, and held her securely.

"No," she said emphatically. "No. I have to go home. There's lots to do. Please take me home." She began to push against him, trying to get down, but his arms were like steel bands. He would have his way.

Chapter 6

"YOU'RE NOT GOING ANYWHERE, little girl," he said so sternly that she stilled and looked up into his no-nonsense face.

"It's time for us to be honest, Annie," said Lukas as he put a finger under her chin to encourage eye contact. "I think we're both feeling things that need to be talked about before we go any further. Agreed?"

Annie considered gathering up the shreds of resistance she was still grasping and using them to steel herself but then remembered the feel of his embrace—the lingering thrill of that kiss—and realized that it was probably hopeless. But she gave it one more try.

"Before we go further? What do you mean? We don't even know each other," she said with more bravado than she felt.

Lukas had to laugh when he said, "No? That's strange. I feel I know a lot about you."

"Do you now?" she said with some attitude. "And what do you think you know?"

"Let's see," he said, lifting her to sit in one of the chairs arranged around a high deck table. "I know that you're kind, intelligent and compassionate." Annie blushed a little but he kept going. "I know you care deeply about your heritage and work hard to preserve it at Oneida Farm. I believe that farm has flourished under your natural leadership qualities and that you'd do just about anything for that place and the people who work there. I also know that you're an amazingly loyal friend to Dyani." Annie had looked away, but he put his hands on the arms of her chair, caging her in and demanded, "Look at me, Annie." When she looked up, he smiled and asked, "How am I doing so far?"

She paused for a moment and said, "I'm flattered that you see those things in me but, Lukas—"

"Oh no. Not finished," he said. "I know that you're independent to a fault and I have also seen you work too hard. I know that in the six months I have known you, you have worked to keep your distance from me though I've patiently tried over and over to scale your wall."

Annie had not thought she was so obvious, but she had to admit he was right. She was touched by his words and also a little stunned. It was hard for her to believe that this head-turning-handsome man who had everything going for him was interested in her. Yet he continued.

"I also know you are one of the most beautiful women I have ever seen, Annie. And I know I want a relationship with you," he said tenderly as he took her face in his hands and stroked his thumbs over her soft cheeks.

Annie could actually feel her heart expand at Lukas' words. All the fences she had worked to build as protection crumbled and Lukas Mattson was walking right in. She was afraid.

Blushing profusely, she managed to say, "I don't know what to say, Lukas." She paused for a moment as she regained her composure. "But I think I also know *some* things about you too," she said, cocking her head, anxious to turn the conversation away from herself.

"Oh, do you now?" he said, standing up straight but still blocking her ability to get down from the chair.

"I know that you are bossy, high handed and… and huge," she said with attitude.

"Hmm," he said, "is that all?"

She looked up into his strong face with those Nordic blue eyes and watched the sun reflect gold lights in his blond hair and she softened. "No, that's not all," she said, folding her hands in her lap shyly. "I know you are well-educated and sophisticated, which makes me wonder why you're interested in me."

He began to interrupt but she said, "No, let me tell you. I know you're a good lawyer, a good investigator, and from what the crew tells me, an excellent hand with the cattle. I wonder what you can't do. I've watched you with groups of young people at the farm and see that you are patient and kind. I know from personal experience that you're brave and…" she blushed and looked down, "… I know you're so good-looking that sometimes when I see you I-I find it hard to breathe." Her face and neck had turned bright red then and all she wanted to do was escape, when Lukas laughed. She loved the deep, rumbly sound of that laugh. She frowned then and said indignantly, "Hey! I'm being painfully honest here and you're laughing at me?"

Lukas took her chin then and said, "I'm not laughing at you, Annie. On the contrary, I'm touched by your words. You're the sweetest girl." She could not really discern the look on his face then, but in the next moment, he slanted his mouth over hers and was kissing her, at first tenderly and then hungrily. Their lips met, and then their tongues, and by the time he pulled away, she felt ready to faint. She surprised him then, by giggling.

"What's so funny, sassy girl?"

"I know another thing about you now. I know that you are the best kisser ever!" she said and giggled again.

"And just how many 'kissers' have you known, Annie?" he asked with mock sternness that covered the jealousy he suddenly felt. When she paused too long, he said again, more seriously this time, "How many, Annie?"

"Wait, I'm counting," she said and giggled again.

Lukas laughed. "Well, I plan to be the last one you'll have for comparison, you little wanton," he said before pressing his mouth to hers again. Her lips parted, inviting him in as his kiss became fiercely possessive. He picked her up as he had earlier and she naturally put her legs around his waist.

"And here we are again, baby—understanding that we know some things about each other and deciding if and how we will go on. But there is more you need to know about me before you commit," he said, moving her to sit back down. She was almost bereft to lose the closeness they had just shared.

With a sigh, she said, "Tell me, Lukas. What else do I need to know?"

He wanted Annie in all ways—body and soul—but he needed to make sure she understood his dominance and what that meant for her.

The sun dipped behind clouds that were gathering and Annie shivered in the breeze.

"Let's go inside," Lukas said, lifting her down from the chair. Annie noticed that, like he had done before, he put his hand on the small of her back as he guided her in the door. She was surprised that she loved the protective gesture. "Sit. I'll get coffee," he said as he indicated the corner of the plush sectional. She sat with her feet curled underneath herself and he reappeared moments later with two warm mugs. He handed her one and sat on the ottoman in front of her and leaned in, his muscled forearms resting on his knees.

Annie smiled up in thanks for the coffee but noticed that his face had become resolute. She decided to make light of it. "You look pretty serious. Have you already decided you don't want to be with me?"

He smiled and shook his head then. "No. It's just that though we know *some* things about each other—there are important things we don't know."

"Okay. Like what?" she asked.

"Like our expectations," he said. "My experience is that success in both professional and personal relationships depend largely on expectations, so I think we need to start there."

"That sounds reasonable. I'm thinking you want to tell me what yours are," she said, taking a sip of her drink.

"Yes," he said as Annie noticed he was a little reticent.

"Lukas, you're right that talking about what we expect from each other is important, though I think most people with successful connections know how to choose their battles and compromise. Are you worried I won't be able to do that?"

"I don't know, Annie. Let me tell you what I need, and you decide, okay?"

She nodded, and Lukas began.

Chapter 7

"I CARE ABOUT YOU, Annie, and that care translates for me into a need to watch over and protect you," Lukas said, watching her face for clues to a reaction. She was listening intently, so he continued. "When you were recovering from the injuries you sustained during the kidnapping, I wanted to make sure you were following doctor's orders and resting. That's why I stopped by every day to check on you. And I can tell you that if you were mine, you would have been more careful during your healing, or there would have been consequences," he said, frowning.

Annie's eyes widened as she considered the words 'if you were mine.' "What do you mean? I don't understand."

"Well, it depends. Remember last night, when you gave me a hard time about changing into pajamas?" he said with his eyebrows raised.

Annie thought back to the smacks he had administered to her bottom and he could see the moment it registered with her. "You mean, if I don't do as you say, you'll *spank* me?" she asked incredulously.

"That would be likely yes," he said, wondering if this was

the moment she would blow up and demand to be taken home. But she didn't—not exactly.

"We're not living in the fifties, Lukas Mattson. What man thinks a woman is 'his' or that he is the boss of her? What man thinks it's okay to spank a woman?"

"This man does," he said, looking at her pointedly. "I believe that it's my responsibility to keep you as healthy and safe as possible, and I have definite ideas about how to do that. I've always been this way and I won't be changing."

Though his words and actions had hinted at his dominant tendency, Annie was still surprised to hear him say it out loud. "I don't understand. What could I possibly do that would make you think I needed 'consequences'? I'm very responsible and organized. Other people rely on me," she said indignantly.

"I'm aware that you have common sense and are generally well-behaved, but I see a weakness in the way you take care—or don't take care of yourself. You take on too much, work longer hours than you should, and don't always eat or sleep well. I watched you push yourself to exhaustion getting the wedding ready in the last few weeks. That's why I decided to just go ahead and bring you up here to rest. I knew you wouldn't do it otherwise. You already look more well-rested today, and I think your stress is diminished. Right?"

Annie wanted to disagree, but in truth, she couldn't remember sleeping as peacefully as she had in the plush bed in Lukas' well-appointed guest room. And not spending the day cleaning up and working on tomorrow's plans was admittedly liberating, so she said with a reluctant sigh, "I do feel much better today and it really is so beautiful and peaceful here." Then, suddenly remembering, she said, "But you took my phone. I don't think that was necessary."

"But I do," he said. "There's nothing going on at the

farm that you need to tend to. Dyani is on her honeymoon and won't be calling. Unplugging is something you can easily do for at least part of a day and I knew you wouldn't do it on your own. I'll give it back later."

"On your timeline?" she asked testily.

"Yup," he said simply.

"And what you decide goes?"

"Yup again, little girl."

"So you're saying that if we're together, I will need to follow your rules or you will hit me?"

"I don't believe in beating or hitting a woman. However, spanking a naughty bottom until it's red is another story. It's usually a pretty good deterrent for risky behavior," he said, squeezing her hands, "and I see it as my responsibility to curb that behavior."

She threw up her hands and said, "You mean I would have to worry all the time about getting spanked?"

"You wouldn't worry all the time because I would make my expectations clear." When she said nothing, he asked, "Are you hearing me, Annie?"

She looked up at him thoughtfully. "Is this the kind of arrangement that Dax and Dyani have? I heard him tell her once that if she didn't call him to tell him when she was leaving for home, she wouldn't sit comfortably for a while."

"I think Dax shares my views, but we've never discussed it. I do know that plenty of couples operate this way and it works out. It's how my parents conducted their marriage and their successful relationship was filled with love and mutual respect until their dying days."

Annie was shaking her head. "I don't know what to say, Lukas. This is all new to me. It sounds like I would need to accept your rules or we couldn't be together. Is that right?"

"That's the way it works with me, Annie." He took her hands then and said, "I want everything between us to be honest. I've never met anyone like you. I think we have something special and I'd like to give us a chance. But I know I am not about to change, so if my dominance is something you can't or won't abide, it's best if we stop now before we hurt each other."

"You *are* very bossy," Annie said with a small smile.

Lukas smiled then too. "I understand that it's a bit old-fashioned and most women usually don't appreciate my nature, but it's who I am and I would want you to understand that before we went forward."

Annie's eyes widened. "When I think of dominant, I think of whips and chains and a dungeon? Is that what you're into?"

Now it was Lukas' turn to be surprised. "No, not at all. And how do you even know about those things?"

"Oh, Lukas, I may be younger than you and raised on the reservation but I am not entirely naive. I read books, see movies, and women talk," she said. "But I'll admit that I don't understand if it's not blindfolds and restraints—what do you mean 'dominant'. Would you be the boss of me?"

"I suppose that would be one way to look at it. Look, Annie, I don't need to control your life but I do need you to be more aware and diligent about caring for yourself. I would insist that you more carefully consider your choices, like decisions about driving safely, not drinking too much, not venturing out at night alone—common sense things."

"And you'd spank me if I didn't choose wisely?" she asked,

He looked directly into her eyes and said, "Yes. I've never given you a real spanking, little girl, but believe me, you'll want to avoid those at all costs. I'm telling you this now so there are no surprises later. Do you understand me?"

"I think so," said Annie, feeling a little overwhelmed.

"I know this is a lot, Annie, but as I said, if we are to commit to this relationship, we need our eyes wide open."

"I agree, Lukas," she said.

"Let me tell you about some things you've done that would not fly if you were mine," Lukas said, sitting up straight.

Annie bit her lip in anticipation of some uncomfortable truths.

Lukas continued. "I've already told you that if we had been together, you wouldn't have gone back to work as quickly as you did after your injuries and you wouldn't have worked so relentlessly on the wedding that you became over-tired. Right?"

Annie nodded.

"And if I had been in your life before the abduction, you wouldn't have complied with the kidnapper's demand that you meet him in an isolated place out in the country."

"I thought I was helping Dyani but it turned out to be a really stupid thing to do," Annie said, quietly lowering her eyes.

He ran his hand through his hair in frustration. "Yeah. I get that. But you would have known better if we had been in a relationship then. You would have known I wouldn't allow you to go out at night alone, and you would also have understood what the consequences would be if you disobeyed me. That might have stopped you, or at least caused you to consider another way."

Annie's eyes grew wide and she squirmed uncomfortably. Lukas thought this was as good a time as any to bring up the incident Adam Skenandore had told him about at the wedding, so he went on. "Did I tell you I met Adam Skenandore last night?"

"No," Annie said nervously.

"He told me about how you protected that young girl

from her abusive boyfriend last year. He said you helped her, and when the punk came to your door, you opened it," Lukas said as his voice rose. "And when he barged in, you threatened him with a gun you apparently keep in the house! Christ, Annie, you could have been killed!" Lukas stood now and was almost roaring at her.

Annie looked up at Lukas from where she sat and, with tears in her eyes, said, "Lukas, he was going to hurt her. And he was white, so he probably would've gotten away with beating her again or even taking her away so that she could never come home again. I did what I had to do!" She gave a choked sob but continued. "And if you told me you would spank me for chasing him off with a gun... well... I'd still do it."

Lukas looked incredulous. Annie didn't know if he was angry or shocked or both. He knew she was right. Legal jurisdiction between tribal and civil law was often murky. Many indigenous women were disallowed justice and ended up in hellish situations. He knew that Annie was known as a strong and smart leader in her community and young women sought her out. This put her in risky circumstances sometimes, but he knew she would never turn away someone in need of help. This would be a difficult dilemma for him. How could he keep her safe when she wouldn't remove herself from dangerous circumstances? He would have to give that a lot of thought. But for now, he realized that he was filled with admiration for the woman that Annie was— beautiful and strong in so many ways.

An entire minute went by before he spoke, and when he did, he sat back down in front of her and gently lifted her onto his lap. He held her and rocked her, saying, "What am I going to do with my brave girl? How can I keep you safe?" Then, after a pause, he said, "Annie, I'm sorry I yelled at you. I understand what you're saying and I promise I'll find a way to help so that you're never in that position again. Do you understand me?"

He turned her in his lap to face him. He arranged her so that her legs straddled his and he put his hands on either side of her face. "You know, baby, I told you what my expectations are but it's a two-way street. Tell me what you need."

Lukas noticed that Annie immediately got a guarded look on her face. She thought for a moment and said, "When I married Elan, I was just eighteen. My grandfather had doubts and was unhappy that he was non-Native. I didn't know what to expect, which was maybe why it took me a while to figure out that I deserved more. He was still a boy and wanted to hang with his friends more than staying home with me. He drank and gambled too much and then I found out he… well, he was unfaithful."

She looked up at Lukas then and said, "I decided then that I had to make my own way, which is why I'm so independent. I'm proud of my self-sufficiency but sometimes I get tired. Sometimes it's all just too much," she said, looking down. "I guess if I had to say what I'd want in a man, it would be for him not to be like Elan—at all. Does that make sense?"

Lukas' heart ached, thinking about Annie being ignored and disrespected. She deserved so much more. This beautiful and strong woman deserved a man who could encourage her in her work and beliefs yet see to her needs, care for her and be a partner.

Holding her face in his hands, Lukas said, "I'm sorry you've been disappointed and hurt before, but I promise you, that if you decide that you can accept me, I'll make sure you are safe and at peace and will honor the strong woman you are." When she didn't respond but seemed to be thoughtfully considering his words, he said, "Listen, I need to go down to Madison until Thursday. Maybe you could take this time to think about what I've told you about how things would be in a relationship with me. There's a lot to think about and maybe with me being gone, you'll be able to think clearly about how you feel. What do you think?"

"Oh, Lukas, I know I care for you, but you're right that I have a lot to consider," she said in an almost pleading tone. "And I need some time." Then she added, "I'll miss you, though."

"I'll miss you, too, babe. I'll want to text or call you when I can so promise me you'll keep your phone charged and on, yeah?"

"I promise," she said. Annie leaned forward and put her face in Lukas' neck. They sat there for a while feeling their hearts beat together and enjoying the soft warmth of their bodies until Annie said, "I've got to get back, Lukas. Can you take me home now?"

"Sure, baby. We'll stop for a sandwich on the way. Go get ready."

In half an hour, they were on their way back to Oneida Farm.

When they pulled up to Annie's house, it was late in the afternoon. Lukas walked her to the door but there seemed to be an unspoken agreement to part ways there. Lifting her chin with his hand, he said, "Promise me you'll ease your way back into work and that you won't be up for hours tonight planning for the week."

"I'll try," she said, looking away.

"No," he said, taking her chin in a stronger grip. "You'll promise or you won't get your phone back."

She stopped herself from stamping her foot in frustration and said, "Okay, Lukas. I promise not to work too hard tonight."

He smiled then, kissed her nose and gave her the phone

back. Then he leaned in to give her a gentle kiss that left her lips tingling and wanting more.

"Be good, baby," he said, giving her a last peck on the top of her head.

Her breath hitched as he turned and she watched that beautiful man get into his truck and drive off. She watched him until the truck was out of sight.

As she walked into her small but homey house, Annie had to admit that the peace and rest Lukas had insisted on had her feeling more relaxed than she had felt in a very long time.

As she fell asleep that night, her head was filled with visions of Lukas She could feel his muscled arms around her, hear his deep voice rumbling in his chest and see the dimple almost hidden in the beard on his rugged face.

Chapter 8

ANNIE'S first day back at the farm was difficult. Autumn and harvest seasons were the busiest times of the year but she had always had Dyani's help. Now, Dyani was on her honeymoon and even when she returned, she would only be at the farm once a week. Issi, the young woman they'd hired to take her place, was capable and helpful, but she was still learning and Annie had to devote time to training her. On Monday, a kindergarten student got too close to a horse who stepped on his foot. Annie accompanied the teacher's aide to Urgent Care and also called the parents to assure them that the boy's foot was not broken and the insurance carried by Oneida Farm would cover the costs. It was a stressful day.

Annie missed Lukas more than she had thought possible. Though she had tried to keep her distance from him since he rescued her months earlier, he had insinuated himself in her life since then and the emptiness she now felt in his absence surprised her, as did the fact that thoughts of him had hijacked her brain, heart—and, to be honest, other body parts—limiting her attention to work and making it difficult to stay on task. Lukas was intelligent, kind and capable. His skill set included everything from handling cattle at the farm to investigating and prosecuting criminal cases in his professional work. And the way he made her tingle with desire every time she saw him—well, the control she prided herself in maintaining disappeared completely!

Lukas' physique exuded masculinity and power from his 6'5" frame and massively broad shoulders to his well-muscled and very sexy backside. Her head swirled with thoughts of his expressive blue-gray eyes, thick head of red-blond hair and brilliant smile that often left her breathless. She had to admit that thinking of his deep voice speaking sternly to her had her panties melting. Remembering the way he kissed her possessively and the way his huge, rough hands felt when he gently held her face or even swatted her bottom, made a heat rise up in her core that was almost overwhelming. Lukas was also tender and caring and perhaps most importantly—she trusted him. Still, she wondered if she could live with his dominant nature. She didn't understand how that would all work—especially the rules and spanking part—but she desperately wanted to find a way.

When he called that night, she almost wept at the sound of his deep and comforting voice but did her best to put on a show of cheerfulness. She talked about her day, trying not to let her stress show through, but Lukas heard the fatigue in her voice and, after a short conversation, insisted she go to bed sooner, rather than later.

"I've got some things to work on yet tonight for a presentation tomorrow for high school students. I can't go to bed yet. Besides, it's only nine o'clock," she said, sounding whiney even to her own ears.

She could hear Lukas make a sound that was between a deep sigh and a growl when he said, "I believe you made me a promise that you wouldn't work too hard. Yeah?"

"I guess I did," she said quietly.

"Damn straight," he said. "You get that little bottom into bed. Now, Annie," he said in a tone that made the idea of arguing seem like a bad one.

And there it was—the responsive tingling in her core that she felt when he spoke that way to her. God help her.

Annie paused for a moment and then said, "Okay, Lukas," and after a brief pause, "I miss you."

"I miss you too," said Lukas tenderly. "I'll be home as early as I can on Thursday night, okay?"

"Okay."

"Good night, baby. Be good."

Annie kept her promise and was in bed in thirty minutes, snuggled under her covers. She wished Dyani was home so she could talk to her about the dilemma of a relationship with a dominant man. Dyani and Dax seemed to have worked things out and were clearly in love. As soon as Dyani got home, she would plan time for a long talk. She had so many strong emotions to sort out. Annie needed her friend.

When Annie rechecked the school group scheduled for Tuesday, she was surprised to find that a third group had been penciled in for the morning. She never scheduled more than two in a half day. She could see it was Issi's handwriting and she was not happy about it. Annie confronted Issi the moment she walked in the door.

"Did you take this call from Pine Ridge Preschool for a tour today?" she asked, trying—but failing—not to sound stressed.

Issi looked over at the calendar and said, "Oh yeah. It's a small group and there seemed to be some time just before lunch to squeeze them in so I told them yes. I love the younger kids. I'll handle it. You don't need to worry." Then she noticed Annie's serious look and said, "You're not upset, are you?"

Annie's annoyance diminished a little when she realized that Issi was so confident in her abilities to handle groups. Annie had watched her work with student groups and she was a natural—especially with preschool children.

"I'm not upset that the group is coming. I'm just used to doing all the scheduling. Three groups are a lot to fit in and I probably wouldn't have done it. I think it will work out but can I ask you to check with me next time?" Annie asked gently, noticing Issi's stricken face.

"I'm sorry. It won't happen again, and as I said, I can handle the group on my own. I know you have lots to do," she said sincerely.

"Thank you, Issi. I know you can do it," said Annie. "And I meant to tell you that the social media posts you put up showing last week's activities at the center were wonderful. We've gotten more response than ever," said Annie, happy to see Issi's face light up with smile and a blush. "Why don't you set up the clipboards for the first group today? It looks like we'll have great weather for a scavenger hunt around the grounds."

Annie had been fond of Issi since she was very young. She was cheerful and always kind to others—even during her teenage years. She had been helping out in small ways at the community center for years and was now becoming a competent assistant to Annie. She knew she should delegate more tasks to Issi and that in order to restore some balance in her life, she would have to ease up on doing everything herself. She knew Lukas would insist on it if they committed to being a couple and while, six months ago, she would have completely resisted his bossy insistence that she follow his lead, she now understood the peace that could come from allowing herself to depend on him—and allowing him to call the shots sometimes. Lukas was a special man in so many ways and Annie knew she was falling in love. Maybe his dominance was something she could learn to handle. Maybe she would come to understand and avoid the things that might push him to deliver "consequences". As she reached that familiar dead end when she considered her "Lukas dilemma", she dragged herself back to the day at hand. She still had a few days before he returned to demand an answer from her. She had to get back to work and focus.

As Annie sat at her desk to do a little paperwork, her phone dinged, and when she checked it, she saw a text from Dyani. "I miss you so much and I really want to talk. Can we facetime later today? Maybe after lunch?"

Annie could feel her heart lift as she typed, "I miss you too. Yes, please call later. Can't wait!"

Chapter 9

LUKAS HADN'T WANTED to leave Annie, but it was necessary. She needed time and space to consider his expectations surrounding his dominance and their future together. The three days of meetings he had scheduled in Madison gave him what he considered an appropriate amount of time for her to process what it would mean to be with him long term. He knew he was in love with her and wanted her. Christ, he'd known that since the first time he saw her beaten and huddled in a corner of a kidnapper's shack. Her beauty got his attention first—jet black waves of shimmering hair down to her waist, the nearly black, almond eyes, and her petite but lush body. Then when he came to know her strength, intelligence and compassionate soul—he was gone. Very worried that a woman of her independence could not accept a man who respected her but required her submission in matters of health and safety, Lukas had trodden lightly, not pushing her on anything—until this last weekend. The wedding was the last straw. It had become torture for him to be near her but not pursue her—not let her know what he needed. And now that she knew, it might be over.

But Lukas had some hope. He knew that Annie was attracted to him and had strong feelings for him as well. And when he had asserted himself over the last few days, allowing his natural dominance to show itself, her reaction had been more compliant than he had expected. There were signs that she might be able to succumb to some submission.

He'd been waiting six months, he could wait a few more days, though no longer. He would have her decision. He had fantasized about making her his, marrying her and beginning a family. However, if she was reluctant to accept his need to take charge or just couldn't do it, he would have to walk away. It would just about kill him, but it was the only way.

———

Lukas hadn't talked to Annie about why he was going to Madison because he wasn't yet sure about where he stood with her. If she decided she wanted to be with him, he would approach her with his idea of establishing a legal and resource center for tribal members at Oneida.

For now, he was exploring his options. The plan he had was in the incubation stage and he needed to talk to some experts and authorities. He wanted his dream to be more of a concrete possibility before he talked to Annie about it.

Working in Green Bay in law enforcement, investigation, and as a lawyer, Lukas had many opportunities to see flaws in the ways the justice system worked—or more often, didn't work—between the state/federal governments and tribal entities. It was a complicated mess and tribal members often suffered in large and small ways from the complex inequities. Women, especially, were left unprotected in cases of divorce, abuse, kidnapping and even murder. If a female tribal member was in a relationship with a non-Native, the tribe's ability to prosecute the non-

Native for abuse and other crimes was hobbled by old state and federal law separating the jurisdictions. An under-funded tribal law enforcement and justice system added to the problem. There were many other factors, but what Lukas saw up close and personal in these cases enraged him, so he had been working the last few years to add specialized knowledge and become educated in tribal law in Wisconsin and how it meshed with state law. He had been taking courses and establishing relationships at the Great Lakes Indigenous Law Center in Madison for a few years now, and though the center was designed to encourage indigenous persons to become immersed in the legal profession, he was accepted there. Lukas has made a name for himself as a knowledgeable resource at the center, given his extensive hands-on background. He was widely respected by students and faculty alike despite the fact that he was non-Native.

After the incident with Dyani and Annie and coming to volunteer at Oneida Farm, Lukas had become even more dedicated to developing a skill set that would enable him to be an asset to First Nation women and men. The story he had learned at the wedding about Annie coming to the aid of a young woman while putting herself at risk brought home the scope of the problems and made it personal.

Recently, Lukas had become involved in his first case concerning a tribal member. About a month ago, a native Oneida Farm laborer—Jake Johnson—was arrested for growing cannabis. He was assigned a public defender but that office was backed up, and as he couldn't afford the $500 bail, he would possibly have to wait in jail for weeks. Jake's co-workers at the farm knew Lukas was a lawyer and asked him for help. Lukas was able to get the charges immediately reduced and paid the bail so Jake could go back to his family and continue to work. Jake ended up paying a doable fine and going on with his life. That act had made Lukas a hero with the crew of men working at Oneida Farm.

Now, Lukas saw that justice for both men *and* women who were tribal members was complex and mired in ancient biases. Real justice was rare. That's when he got an idea.

Lukas truly enjoyed the volunteer work he did with the cattle crew at Oneida, and through his relationship with Annie, he had come to respect native culture even more. It occurred to him that he could make a more meaningful difference in the lives of those in Annie's beloved Oneida tribe by providing legal services as well as helping them navigate their options for services for which they were eligible by virtue of their heritage. Lukas was financially secure, not needing to work for a salary, so he could provide his services pro bono and could begin small, with a legal center on the grounds of Oneida Farm. He would need to set up a nonprofit and get some funding and talent to help. He was loathe to pursue government funding—at least at first—as he had his own ideas about how a legal center would operate. But he would want permission and support from government entities including law enforcement. It would require a lot of connecting—a lot of work on relationships. Lukas was good at that, and so was Annie.

By the time he left Annie to go to Madison for meetings with those whom he thought might back his plan, he had more than an outline of what he wanted to do. In fact, he had designed what he thought was a viable and detailed business plan and mission statement. He was eager to get the opinions of the people at the Great Lakes Indigenous Law Center. He really wanted to establish his pilot plan with the Oneidas and he was dying to share the idea with Annie, but he had to know if she really wanted to commit to a relationship with him, going forward.

Lukas steered his thoughts from Annie and dedicated the

evening to readying his plan for presentation and reading more research. He was able to fall asleep, but in his dreams, he saw her smile, felt the curve of her hips as they danced, and relived the tantalizing kiss they had shared.

He woke in the morning with a raging hard-on and renewed motivation to get his pilot program off the ground.

Chapter 10

ANNIE WAS able to arrange some alone time in her office to wait for Dyani's facetime call while she nibbled on some lunch snacks. She rarely got an actual "lunch hour" or even half hour, as there was always something she felt she had to attend to at the farm.

She didn't have long to wait. Dyani called at twelve-thirty, and though they had seen each other just days ago at the wedding, so much had changed. Annie was so happy to see her friend's face and hear her voice that tears pricked her eyes.

"Oh, Dynai, I'm so happy to see you!" said Annie, noticing that Dyani looked more happy—even radiant—than she remembered. "You look so happy, even at peace."

"It's so dreamy up here, Annie. The house is almost solid windows, so there are nature views at every angle and in every room, so even when it rained yesterday, I still felt like I was part of the outside world. And it's so quiet! Dax's place is set apart from the tourist areas, and this time of year, very few people take the ferry over here. It's like heaven—except that even though I was officially married before last weekend, things seem more real now. I feel like there has never been a time when I didn't love Dax with all of my being. It's almost overwhelming," she said as tears glistened in her eyes.

"I'm so happy for you, Dyani. You deserve true love," said Annie with heartfelt affection for her friend.

"The only thing even a little sad is that I miss you so much!"

Annie smiled at Dyani's happy stream of consciousness. "I miss you too—in so many ways—but I love knowing that you've found the man you love and that he feels the same way. I'll never forget the way he looked at you all day Saturday. He had eyes for no one else."

At that, Dyani giggled and said, "Well, I noticed that Lukas has eyes for no one else, either. Have you finally decided to let him into your life?" When Annie actually blushed, Dyani squealed and said, "Oh, something happened! I just know it! Tell me—please!"

Annie told her friend the entire story about how Lukas had arranged for all the clean-up work to be done by the Farm interns and had insisted she leave with him when he thought she was tired. She told her how he didn't give her a choice and took her to his house instead of home and bullied her into relaxing, napping and sleeping most of the weekend. She was indignant when she told Dyani that he even took her phone away.

"Oh my gosh! That sounds so much like Dax," said Annie, but as it suddenly occurred to her that Annie was no pushover and was unlikely compliant, she asked, "How do you feel about that?"

Annie paused and then said quietly, "I don't know—I mean I have conflicting feelings about it—big conflicting feelings."

"That sounds hard, Annie. Do you want to talk about it?" Dyani asked gently.

"It's difficult to talk about, but I need you, Dyani. I think you'll understand." Annie's voice was almost pleading. Then she said, "Dax isn't right there, is he? I only want to talk with you."

"He went to check on our neighbors, an old couple who live up here all year round. He said he may do some work for them if they need it, so he's gone for now. Don't worry, Annie. I'm here for you and I'll keep what you tell me in my heart."

Thinking about what a dear friend she had in Dyani, Annie said, "Okay, here goes."

Annie began by telling Dyani how she was reluctant and even fought her feelings for Lukas, but how he had slowly and methodically worked his way into her life and how her feelings then became unmanageable. She talked to Dyani about how her attraction for him had grown into affection, admiration, and now she thought—well, she thought she was in love.

Dyani told her that she had suspected as much but didn't want to interfere. "I'm thinking that the "love" thing is making you feel out of control, and I know that's hard for you. Right?"

"Oh, so right! You do know me," said Annie, relieved to see that Dyani understood her so well. She decided to go ahead and tell her about the dilemma. "The weekend was magical, Dyani. Lukas was right that I needed rest, and it felt wonderful. He fed me, built fires and generally catered to all my needs. I've never taken time off in that way or been so pampered," Annie said dreamily. "And that kiss!"

Dyani's voice hitched. "Kiss?"

"I never knew… I didn't know… it was so amazing. I never wanted it to stop."

There was pause then before Dyani asked, "And is there more?"

"There's more, but not what you think. What I didn't tell you is that all the while Lukas was pampering me, he was somehow also the most bossy man I've ever known." Now, Annie sounded miffed. "He ordered me around, Dyani!"

"Did he now?" her friend asked, trying to sound like she was commiserating. "How so?"

Annie told her about how Lukas had suddenly gone all take-charge on her, dictating everything from where to shower to what to eat to how long to sleep. She repeated angrily that he had also taken her phone—something that really pushed her buttons.

"And then, when I didn't immediately comply with the huge oaf, he threatened to spank me! He even swatted me a few times when I refused to change into pajamas!"

"That made you angry?" Dyani asked, evenly holding back what she really wanted to say.

Annie paused. "That's the problem. I *was* mad, but I realized that I had never felt so safe and cared for as I did when Lukas took care of me. I began to think it was worth it and actually… it sort of turned me on." That last part was said so quietly that Dyani barely heard it, but she understood. Before she could answer, Annie wailed, "What is the matter with me? I am strong and independent. I've been on my own for a while now and I could do everything by myself. Why is this alpha male thing suddenly okay with me—more than okay?" She paused again and Dyani let her continue. "And more importantly, Lukas told me that even though he wants a relationship with me, I would need to understand that he is dominant. He says it's the way he has always been and he's not likely to change. He talked about me following rules—rules—like I'm a child! He said if I didn't, or if I ever defied or lied to him, he would spank me. He said we could always talk first but if he deemed it necessary, he would spank me, Dyani!" Annie was now worked up, so Dyani knew she needed to calm her down.

"Oh, my dear Annie," Dyani said compassionately. "I understand that you're in such a dilemma. I'm sorry. Can I help?"

"I hope so," Annie said, sighing. "Dyani, this is difficult for me to say, but I believe you and Dax have a relationship at least a little like what Lukas is describing to me. I need to know if that's true and how you handle it. I just don't know if I can. Lukas left for Madison until Thursday and wants me to think about it and give him an answer when he comes back," Annie said as she began to sob. "I don't know what to do. I think I love him. I want him. I want a relationship with him, but can I make it work with a dominant man? I don't know!"

Dyani's heart ached for Annie. She knew it would be even more difficult for her to accept a powerful and assertive man like Lukas than it had been for her to understand Dax. She knew she couldn't make light of it or just offer platitudes, so she thought carefully about her next words. "It sounds like there are many things about Lukas to like—even admire and love, right?"

"I've never met a man like him before. I didn't know they existed. Sometimes I can't believe he is even interested in me," said Annie with a little wonder in her voice.

"I understand," said Dyani. "So the fact that he is bossy and says he will deliver consequences for some behavior is what's holding you up?"

Annie was quiet for a least a full minute. "Yes. It's holding me up. I have not had to answer to anyone for such a long time and I am proud of my self-sufficiency," she said, feeling less sure than she had before. "But, on the other hand, when he talks sternly to me, and even when he threatens me with a spanking to insist I take care of myself, I feel so safe—so protected. It's the strangest thing. Is there something wrong with me?"

"No. There's nothing wrong with you. You are strong, competent and independent and giving over some control to someone else, even someone as otherwise perfect as Lukas Mattson, is difficult for you. I guess I'd be surprised if you didn't resist," Dyani said thoughtfully. "Everyone is different, but I can tell you that when I realized that Dax was a Dom, I didn't know what to think. But over time, I came to understand that this is one of the ways he loves me. It became a dynamic I not only could accept, but wanted."

"You want him to spank you?" Annie asked incredulously.

"No. No, I never want it. When Dax resorts to a spanking, he means business—he means to make a memorable impression on me. And it does," she said definitely. "But when it's over, I feel more safe than I have ever felt in my life. I can depend on Dax in all things, including paying attention to and caring what I do. It's part of how he loves me, Annie, and I accept that love. And, really, I understand him and what he needs so much better now. I know what will push his buttons and I try not to do it. Spankings are few and far between. It works for us, but you will have to see if it works for you and Lukas."

"You make a lot of sense, Dyani. But I can't just say to him 'okay, go ahead and spank me when you think it's necessary'. I think he wants me to give him permission," Annie said.

"It's not really permission, but rather that he just wants to know that it won't be a dealbreaker. Does that make sense?" Dyani asked.

Just then, Issi knocked on the office door and Annie signaled her to wait just a minute.

"Listen, I have to go, but you've been so much help. I

have a lot to think about, but you've given me new ways to do that. You are such a good friend," Annie said sincerely. "I can't want to see you again."

"You've been a dear friend to me, Annie, and I love you. I want the best for you. I know this is difficult, but know that I am always here for you. And we'll be home on Saturday. Maybe I can see you this weekend. Let's try to work it out."

"Absolutely," said Annie. "Enjoy the rest of your peaceful week together. I'll see you soon. Bye, Dyani."

Annie put down her phone and let out a big sigh as she welcomed a feeling of resolution. She knew she would be thinking deeply about all the things Dyani said and returned to work feeling like a heavy weight had been lifted from her. She was filled with hope.

Chapter 11

WHEN LUKAS TALKED with Annie on Tuesday night, he could tell there was something different in her demeanor. She cheerfully told him all about her day at Oneida Farm and how well Issi was working out. She sounded happy, and when she told him how much she missed him and how she couldn't wait to see him again, he was encouraged. She didn't sound like a woman who had decided to give up on their relationship.

Lukas didn't tell her much about why he was in Madison or how it was going because he was still working on final plans. His meetings on Wednesday could make or break the project. But he did tell her that things were going well and he was pleased about it. He told her that he'd be home on Thursday after work. He'd call during the day with details. When he reminded her that he wanted her in bed by 10:00, she surprised him by replying, "Yes, Lukas." Oh, things were definitely looking up.

Things continued looking up on Wednesday after a meeting with a dean from the Great Lakes Indigenous Law Center, the executive director of the Center for Health

Progress, whose program concerning justice for indigenous women had gained regional reknown, and a representative from Wisconsin's Tribal Affairs office. Dan Cornelius, an old friend of Lukas' who had been the only indigenous detective on the Green Bay Police Dept. and now worked as a liaison between tribal and local law enforcement, had been able to get Wisconsin's Attorney General to attend the meeting to hear Lukas' proposal. He was a big 'get' and Lukas was grateful to Dan.

Dan and Lukas had met the night before and decided that it would be best if they co-presented the pilot. Dan tactfully pointed out to Lukas that while he was well-respected and admired, he was not native. In fact, his physical appearance could not be more opposite and could appear intimidating. Dan explained that the proposal would carry more weight and seem more credible with tribal leaders if they worked together and Dan was eager to see the program's success.

Dan was right. The presentation about setting up a pro bono legal center for Oneida tribal members staffed with a lawyer, an investigator and social services referral agency was enthusiastically received. Those in attendance all agreed that making collaboration between tribal and local and state law enforcement and justice systems the cornerstone of the organization could lead to a better life for so many tribal members.

The morning meeting that was scheduled for ninety minutes lasted through lunch, as there was much brainstorming and a healthy exchange of ideas. When the meeting concluded early in the afternoon, the Attorney General praised Lukas and Dan and committed his office to be available to help in any way.

Lukas was thrilled and couldn't wait to share everything with Annie. He decided not to stay one more night and, instead, leave for Oneida right away. He wanted to surprise Annie with his early return.

He had to tamp down the mental image he held of her asleep on a bed in his guest room with her dress scrunched up to reveal her long, lithe legs, her stunning, bright black hair fanned out over pillows and blankets, and her lush lips swollen in sleep. It took everything he had to divert his thinking so he didn't speed unreasonably as he made his way to her.

———

Wednesday had been relatively slow at Oneida Farm and Annie was able to send Issi home around two o'clock. She reasoned that it would give her some quiet time to do paperwork and scheduling, but since her conversation with Dyani the day before, her brain and heart were brimming over with thoughts of Lukas, her magnificent Viking. Besides the fact that his looks had her melting each time she saw him, he was so much more—intelligent, kind and funny. She loved every minute with him, even when he was being the boss of her and speaking sternly in the incredibly sexy voice. After her talk with Dyani, she felt she could give herself permission to love everything that was Lukas Mattson and to begin to accept his dominance. She was anxious to tell him that she wanted to go forward with him and was willing to try. She could feel her reluctance slipping away.

As she gave up on accomplishing anything and began to close up the building, she heard the bell on the front door ring. She made her way to the front door and saw a young woman holding the hand of a little boy who was maybe about three. As she approached them, she could see that the woman looked anxiously over her shoulder and the little boy was begging her to pick him up. When she opened the door, she saw that the young woman had bruises on her face, including a black eye.

Annie schooled herself to react calmly and welcomed them by saying, "Come and sit down next to the pellet stove, it's still warm," she said, directing them to the comfortable seating area near the stove. "Can I get you some water?"

The little boy said, "Juice. I want juice."

His mother tried to shush him but Annie smiled and crouched down to talk. "Sure thing. What would you like, apple or grape?"

"Apple juice! Apple juice," he said, clapping his hands.

Annie stood. "I'm Annie, the director here," she said kindly, looking into the tired eyes of the young woman.

Quietly, the woman said, "I'm Laney, and this is my son, Thomas." Then, with her eyes darting toward the door fearfully, she said in almost a whisper, "We need some help."

"I understand," said Annie and then said, "Thomas, let's go pick out the juice you want out of that refrigerator there." The little boy took Annie's hand and pranced excitedly next to her as they retrieved juice and water. Annie then led him to the play area, hoping she could talk more privately with his mother. When Thomas seemed settled, Annie sat down next to Laney and said, "It looks like you walked here today. You must be tired. How can I help you?"

Laney stole a glance at her little boy and said quietly, "My husband… he said… he said he would kill me if I tried to leave. But I can't stay. He's always drunk, and this morning, he hit my head so hard, I passed out." Annie put her hand over Laney's hand as she continued. "When I finally came to, Thomas was hiding in his closet, crying, and Jed— my husband—had left and taken our car and my phone. I knew I had to get out of there. I'm desperate!" She paused to take a deep breath. "I heard you help people, so we walked here." Trying not to break down, she added, "I'm so sorry. I didn't know what to do. I can't go back."

Annie put her arm around the other woman's shoulders and said, "You did the right thing. We'll figure things out."

Annie began to wrack her brain for a plan. They needed a safe place to go and time was of the essence, as her husband had said he would come after her. If he did, she— and the boy—were in danger. It was getting dark and if he followed them here, she would be on her own, as everyone had already left for the day.

Her first idea was to call the women's domestic abuse shelter in Green Bay. She had a friend there. But when Annie went to grab her phone from behind the counter, she saw that it had no charge. That was a bad habit she had and she knew Lukas would not be happy about it. She excused herself to her office to use the landline there and called the shelter, but sadly, her friend said they were full, actually, more than full for tonight. She suggested another shelter, but it was not one for domestic abuse victims and wouldn't be secure enough if Jed followed them. The police would come to take a statement and begin the process of obtaining a restraining order, but unless her husband was here presenting a clear danger, they couldn't help. Annie wasn't sure if Laney would even press charges. That sometimes made things worse. The only thing Annie could think to do now was to take her home with her. Annie's house was isolated out in the country and Laney's husband would have no idea where to look. Maybe tomorrow, they could search for a domestic abuse shelter down in the Fox Valley. Annie wished Lukas was here but decided if she called him, there wouldn't be much more he could do than she had and it would take him a couple of hours to get home from Madison. He wouldn't like the idea of her taking the chance of sheltering Laney and Thomas, but she didn't see another way. She'd deal with Lukas when he returned tomorrow.

Annie walked back into the main community room and saw Thomas quietly playing with toy trucks on the floor near his mother. Laney had her head in her hands, presenting a forlorn picture. This kind of situation was sadly common for indigenous women, especially those whose partners were non-Native. It never failed to enrage Annie who sat down next to Laney and began to explain that she would have to take them to her home.

That's when they heard the sound of car with a deafeningly loud muffler pull up to the building.

"It's Jed!" said Laney in a hoarse whisper so as not to alarm Thomas. "He'll take Thomas!"

"No. He won't. Come with me," said Annie as she calmly led them to the door to the basement of the center. As Jed began pounding on the door yelling for his wife, Annie put her hands on Laney's narrow shoulders and said, "Listen to me. There's a secure room in the back corner of the basement. Take Thomas and lock yourself in. I'm going to call the police and hold him off until they get here." Annie opened the door and turned on the light. "It will be okay, Laney. Just stay as quiet as you can, okay?" she said as she looked into the woman's terrified face.

Jed was still pounding relentlessly on the door and bellowing for Laney while Annie frantically got to the landline phone and dialed 911. She had just given her name and address when she noticed the pounding had stopped and it was eerily quiet. Annie completed her emergency call and moved toward the front of the room when, suddenly, there was the sound of glass shattering. She saw that a large rock had broken a window—a window that had a man climbing in.

"Where the fuck are they?" Jed snarled. "Laney! Thomas, it's Daddy. Where are you?"

"I don't know who you're talking about. There's no one here. Get out," Annie said, running into the room and bravely standing her ground, though he now stood in her space confronting her with his teeth bared and his breath laden with alcohol.

"Get out of my way, bitch. I know they're here,"

When she lifted her chin defiantly, Jed raised his arm and viciously backhanded her while growling, "I'll kill you, bitch!"

Annie curled into a protective position on the floor with her legs drawn up and her arms shielding her face. She waited for the next hit or kick—but it didn't come. She heard the front door crash open and when she peeked up at her assailant, she saw a fist connect with his jaw and he was suddenly sprawled unconscious on the floor as Lukas stood over him.

"Lukas! How did you… When did you… Oh, thank God!" exclaimed Annie as she tried to stand but found herself unsteady as Lukas scooped her up to sit her on the sofa.

"Annie, baby, where does it hurt?" he asked as he gently examined her body for injuries, finally settling on her face which was red and swollen. There was some blood coming from her split lip. "Are you hurt anywhere else?"

When she shook her head, he kissed her forehead and asked, "What happened here? Who is this asshole?"

As Annie opened her mouth to speak, they heard sirens nearby and within seconds, two armed officers were breaking through the door with Annie's boss right behind them.

Lukas pointed to Jed and said, "I got here just in time to see this guy attack Annie, so I took him down. I only got in one punch so he'll be coming around anytime. Better restrain him. Jason, get an ice pack for Annie's face."

It pained Annie to speak, but she said, "Wait, they're in the back room—in the basement. They were running for him. Please let me go to them. They're scared." She tried to get up but Lukas held her firm.

"Annie, who's in the basement? Tell me."

"Laney and her little boy. They came here trying to get away from her husband. They walked so far! He said he'd kill her and take Thomas away," she said, looking up at Lukas. "Then he was here pounding on the door and I hid them in the basement. He broke a window and got in. I couldn't let him find them, Lukas! He was angry and he hit me," she said, crying now. "And then you were here, Lukas. You came! You saved us!"

He wrapped his arms around her and rocked her gently, saying, "I got you, baby. You're okay. I'm here." Then he called out to Jason, "Do you know what room she's talking about?"

"I do. I'll go get them," Jason said, heading for the basement door.

"No! No!" Annie said, wriggling out of Lukas' arms. "They're frightened, but they know me. Let me go down," she said, standing up. Then she looked over at Jed who was restrained but beginning to gain consciousness. "Can you get him out of here? Seeing his daddy like this will upset Thomas—and Laney. Who knows what he'll say."

"Good idea, baby," and then to the officers, he said, "can you read him his rights and get him out of here? We'll give a statement later."

Annie went to reassure Laney and Thomas and bring them up. Lukas watched as Annie came into the room holding the hand of a frightened little boy. His mother followed close behind, looking traumatized. Annie was able to distract Thomas with toys and go to sit with an arm around his mother's shoulders, speaking quietly. Lukas was once again amazed at Annie's ability to lead and comfort in difficult situations. His admiration for her continued to grow —as did his love.

One of the officers came in and, looking to Lukas, asked, "Do you think we can get some statements? We'll need them to keep her husband in jail for a while." Lukas nodded. It was going to be long night.

Chapter 12

ONE WEEK LATER...

It was indeed a long night, and that was followed by a long week. Annie knew she would look back at the past week and wonder how she had ever handled the overwhelming number of complicated issues that had her on an emotional roller coaster.

First, the ordeal of Jed's break-in, assault, and attempt to kidnap Thomas presented a very complex set of problems involving legal issues between tribal and civic entities. Jed was non-Native and that often allowed some escape loopholes for accountability. And then, when there was a child involved, it became more difficult. Getting restraining orders in place with urgency in mind and finding secure temporary shelter for mothers and children added to the challenges faced by Laney and her son. Most indigenous women who did not have the resources to hire the specialized lawyers needed to protect their rights found themselves right back in the trap of lives they did not control and that were sometimes violent.

But Laney and Thomas were in the right place at the

right time. Not only had Lukas Mattson happened to come home early and walk right into a volatile domestic conflict, but the circumstances in this case were the very same issues that Lukas had been preparing for and had decided to make his life's work. He was already extremely well-versed in the legal issues between cultures and had now gotten support from tribal leaders, state legislators and women's rights groups to create his pilot legal center at Oneida.

Then there was the issue Annie was facing concerning her position at Oneida Farm. She loved working there and had assumed she would spend her working life there educating others about her heritage and being a leader in her close community.

But that was before Lukas and before they had the opportunity to work as a team to rescue Laney and set her on the track for a better life going forward. Lukas had been able to handle all the legal matters that allowed Laney to begin divorce proceedings and set up a very limited and highly supervised visitation schedule for Jed to see Thomas—and that would begin only after Jed had served a three-year sentence. This would not have been possible for Laney if Lukas had not been there and then donated his work.

Annie, for her part, had used strong connections she had in the Oneida tribe and also with some women at the nearby Menominee Family Center to procure safe temporary shelter for Laney. She was also able to hook her up with programs that provided free child care and tuition to a nearby technical college for two years.

It was clear Lukas and Annie made for an effective partnership and he wanted her to join him in this new endeavor. Jason Metoxen, her boss, had arranged to cover for Annie during the week when all her attention and energy needed to be devoted to Laney and Thomas. He told her that if she wanted to join Lukas in his work, the decision was hers and that she was free to go if and when she felt ready. Jason understood it to be the opportunity of a lifetime. But it was not easy. She needed time to think and time to work out details.

Lukas and Annie had very little time alone together during the week since the attack and both had been working to near exhaustion, as many of the issues needed handling quickly. But now, a week later, they finally had some time for themselves. Lukas persuaded Annie to come home with him to Brussels over the weekend. He hoped they would have time to process what had happened and, more importantly, talk about their future together. She fell sound asleep on the way to his home, and when they got there, he made her a sandwich and bundled her off to bed—*in a guest room*. She was disappointed but just too tired to argue.

———

Annie woke early, as she usually did—before dawn—and when she couldn't get back to sleep, she got up and quietly showered and dressed. She was surprised not to hear signs of life from Lukas' bedroom and couldn't wait any longer. She poured a glass of juice and tiptoed into his bedroom, where the early light of day allowed her to appreciate the magnificent naked man lying spread out on his back on the enormous bed that had been custom made for the giant he was. Annie curled up in the overstuffed chair in the corner of his bedroom and began to mentally tick off all the parts of him that she found incredibly hot.

Lukas' thick red/gold hair messily framed his face and neck. It was a decidedly more wild look than when it was pulled back in a neat warrior style knot on most days. Annie loved his beard, even when he had not had time this week to give it the attention of a trim. Again, it added to the wild vibe she loved. Lukas's face was craggy and rugged, with a strong jaw and pronounced cheekbones. She had never seen shoulders as broad as his, and the well-defined muscles of his lightly haired chest began to make her tingle. Suddenly, he rolled slightly to his side. Annie froze but he didn't wake. Instead, he gave her a view of his tight, masculine butt, which was so sexy, her breath hitched. Lukas' legs were like tall tree trunks, and she even found his feet somehow attractive. Just looking at him, had heat rising from her core. At this rate, she would have to change her panties. Annie was having so much fun with this game of secretly admiring all his sexy parts that she put down her glass and very carefully moved around the bed to observe him from another angle. The first thing she saw was his cock, which had obviously come awake before he did. She knew that men often got hard in the morning, but did all men have cocks of this intimidating size? She was fascinated and couldn't look away. She was becoming so aroused that without realizing it, she drew closer and closer to the side of the bed until, suddenly, a giant hand snaked out and grabbed her wrist, and in his rough, early-morning voice, Lukas said, "Like what you see, baby girl?"

Annie had been caught completely off guard as evidenced by the blood-curdling scream she emitted. "You scared me to death, Lukas! That was so mean! How could you do that to me?" she cried, trying to catch her breath and pull away from him. When he threw his great head back and began to laugh, she batted at him indignantly. By now, she was blushing furiously, trying to hide her face and still attempting to get away.

"I hate you, Lukas Mattson. I just hate you!" she said as tears threatened, and try as she might not to cry, that's exactly what she did.

Lukas stopped laughing and pulled her to him in one

movement. He had her tightly held in his arms, facing him on the bed. She was still struggling, but when he said soothingly, "Oh, I'm sorry, baby. I didn't mean to scare you."

She raised up on her elbow and said angrily, "Like hell, you didn't! How long were you watching me?"

"Not as long as you were apparently watching me," he said, chuckling.

That took the wind out of her sails and she lay back down, looking into his smiling face. She had to smile then but put a hand over her embarrassed face.

"You're right. I *was* looking at you for a long time and… and I *did* definitely like what I saw," she said, peeking up at him.

"Why, Annie Summerhill, I believe you are trying to seduce me," he said, running a huge hand gently down her back to rest on her bottom. That act made her clench inside and she knew she was lost.

Peeking up at him again, she asked, "Is it working?"

"Now you're playing with fire, baby," he said, reaching down and placing one rough finger inside her folds. "Ah, and you're already damn hot and wet, aren't you?"

He began to stroke her clit then and she gasped, loudly crying out, "Oh, Lukas, please. Pleeeease."

"I've got this, baby. Relax. I'm driving," he growled into her ear. When she grabbed the bottom of her shirt to take it off, he immediately flipped her over and delivered several hard smacks to her bottom, saying, "You know the rules here, baby. I'm in charge, yeah?"

Crying out and gasping at the sting, she said, "I'm sorry, Daddy. I'll be good."

Her use of that meaningful endearment had Annie surprised at herself and Lukas thinking he'd died and gone to heaven.

"That's right, baby girl. You let Daddy undress you, and

when you've been naughty, you call me Daddy. I'm in charge and I'll spank your bottom raw if you forget," he said with his eyes turning dark and his lust barely controlled.

At his words, Annie's body thrummed with desire. How could he understand that secret need she harbored? The need sometimes to let go—to give over—to let him take over. She didn't even understand how his dominance—even just stern talking—unlocked doors of passion inside her. Doors she hadn't even known were closed in the first place.

Lukas yanked her arms over her head and used the t-shirt to trap her hands together.

"Don't move those hands unless I tell you, understand?" he said and then dragged his rough hands all the way down her body. When he got to her flat belly, he began to kiss and lick his way upwards, stopping to suckle each nipple until it was erect and needy. Annie groaned and began to squirm. In a flash, he had raised her thigh and given her a smack so hard, the sound of it reverberated in the room. She let out a cry, but he said, "Lie still, naughty girl, or I won't let you come. Is that what you want?"

"No, Daddy, no!" she pleaded desperately. "I mean, please. Please."

"What do you want, baby?" he asked, chuckling softly into her ear.

"I want you! All of you! Please, Daddy!"

"Christ, Annie, you're so beautiful. You make me wild," he said, reaching into the nightstand to produce a condom.

He was just about to rip the wrapper with his teeth when Annie said breathlessly, "No need. I'm on the pill."

Lukas smiled in an almost dark way and grabbed her ankles to put them over his shoulders. "That's good, baby. I want to feel you—every part of you."

He moved over her then, taking her mouth in a devouring kiss that had their tongues tangling and their breathing hard and raspy. Lukas' cock was like granite and though he had wanted to take things slower, he couldn't hold on. He lost control with her. Lukas reached down to her clit, stroking it and finding her more than ready for him. She moaned loudly and then when he teased her with the head of his cock, she began to beg and thrash her head. Still holding her wrists above her head, he began to move into her, slowly at first, until she adjusted to him.

"Oh God, Lukas! I've never—you're so big—oh, it feels so good!" Annie called out breathlessly. Her loud moans of pleasure encouraged him and he could tell she was close.

"Come for me, baby. Daddy wants his little girl to come," he said, straining as he felt his own orgasm unfurling. Suddenly, he felt her clench around him as she made incoherent sounds of passion. He let go of her hands and thrust again and again as she grabbed for his back and dug her nails into him. Feeling her ride her wave of ecstasy, he knew when she peaked, and that caused him to go over the top and pump copious amounts of his seed into her while calling out her name in an almost animalistic growl.

Annie wound her legs and arms around him so tightly, there was no space between their bodies. They were as one as they experienced the aftermath of their epic coupling. Lukas rolled Annie to his side, pushing wet strands of hair off her face and whispering endearments as he caught his breath. Still inside her, he continued to feel her muscles spasming around his cock and thought he could die happy right then. He had never experienced an orgasm of that magnitude.

"I love you, Lukas Mattson," said Annie, sounding breathy and spent.

"And I love you, Annie Summerhill," he said, gently separating from her as he kissed her face, neck and collarbone. "You're mine."

Annie smiled sleepily and snuggled her face into Lukas' neck, relishing the feel of his muscular chest under the layer of fine hair. She now thought of him as her love—her hero —her Nordic god. She felt she could stay like this forever.

Then her stomach growled—loudly—and she heard Lukas' laugh vibrating through her.

Chapter 13

ANNIE BLUSHED AND SAID, "Oh, excuse me. I must be more hungry than I thought. Let me..." She moved to get up but Lukas held her.

"Stay right there," he ordered and went to the bathroom where he cleaned himself up and brought a warm cloth out to gently wash away the evidence of their lovemaking. "Go get dressed while I make something to put into your complaining stomach." She smiled, and as she ran back to the bedroom where he had put her the night before, he called, "Later on, I want you to bring all of your things in here where they belong—where *you* belong. Do you hear me?"

"I hear you, Daddy," she said, giggling, and he knew he would never tire of the sound of her giggle—or the sound of her calling him Daddy.

It was the first really chilly morning of October, so when Annie entered the kitchen to the homey smells of eggs and bacon, she was wearing an oversized, soft turtleneck sweater that was black and matched the leggings covering her petite legs. He noticed her feet were bare so he simply said, "Socks or slippers."

"What?" she asked, confused.

"It's cold this morning and your feet will get cold." When she just stared up at him, he put down the spatula, grabbed her shoulders to turn her and swatted her bottom. "Socks. Now. Go."

Annie stomped her foot but was back in a moment wearing bright pink striped socks. She plopped down in the chair with some attitude but Lukas just chuckled and put her breakfast down in front of her. They ate their eggs and toast in companionable silence, but then Lukas wiped his mouth and announced, "We need to talk. Go get comfy by the fireplace and I'll bring you some coffee."

Annie was pretty sure that Lukas didn't even know how bossy he was—it was just part of him. He rarely asked her anything, but rather told her how things were going to go. In the beginning, she found that habit extremely annoying, but now that she knew what to expect from him, she could generally accept it. Sometimes she found it oddly comforting and even more oddly arousing.

She settled in cross-legged on the soft down cushions of the large sectional in Lukas' great room and took the mug of coffee he gave her. He sat on an ottoman in front of her with his elbows on his knees, looking at her. "That's a pretty serious look you have on your face, Lukas. I wonder if I'm going to like what you have to say," she said lightly.

His expression didn't change and he said, "I think you'll like some of the things I need to tell you and others… well, not so much. But it's all important, so I need you to listen, yeah?"

"I understand," she said. "I'm listening, Lukas."

He began by telling her how proud he was of the work she had done the past week in getting Laney and Thomas settled. "You took care of the things I wouldn't know anything about or would not have thought of, like arranging child care and other programs available to indigenous women. I've seen the knowledgeable and professional way you handle things at the farm, but this was a new environment and you rose to the occasion impressively. I don't think anyone could have done a better job," he said sincerely. "The help you provided allowed me to do my thing. We make a good team, Annie, doing just the kind of work I'm hoping to do when I get the legal center going," he added, reaching out to rest his warm hand on her knee.

Annie blushed, smiled, and quietly said, "Thank you."

He smiled and asked, "Can you tell me what you're thinking about all of this?"

Annie put her hand over his and said, "Well, I've seen so many women and children who have been in situations like Laney, and I know that a very small percentage are able to escape their quiet desperation. The women here have never had the help of someone like you. We can't afford adequate legal representation, and even if we could, I don't know of anyone with your expertise who is able to navigate the complexities of tribal and civic law when dealing with family issues." She lowered her eyes then, not sure how to go on, but he lifted her chin with his knuckle and saw tears in her eyes. She tried to continue. "It's really nothing short of a miracle that you, a non-Native, actually want to do this work. You're a knight in shining armor, Lukas Mattson, and I am in awe of you." Lukas brushed away a tear that had escaped her eye and coursed down her cheek. "I love you."

"The feeling is mutual, baby—I'm awestruck and in love with you as well. We definitely have something special going on here. Besides a personal relationship, we may also be successful professionally," he said, squeezing her hands. He paused then and took a deep breath.

"I sense a 'but' coming," Annie said warily.

Lukas' eyes flew to hers and he was struck by her intuition as he said, "Yeah, there's a 'but'. Listen to me. I know you're strong, smart, filled with empathy and too beautiful for words. I love those things about you. *But* you are also compulsive, stubborn, and risk taking."

Unable to sit any longer, Lukas stood, ran a hand over his face and beard and began to pace in front of her. With his voice becoming more tense and frustrated, he said, "You put yourself in harm's way. You seem to have little common sense about keeping yourself safe. You don't lock doors, or keep your phone charged, or let others know where you are and when you're going to be alone." Annie bit her lip to keep from crying as Lukas continued to scold. What had begun as a loving conversation was going off the rails. "Christ, Annie. It's impossible for me to see you in danger or hurt. Do you know how I felt when I saw Jed attacking you? I lost my mind! I felt completely helpless. There have to be some guard rails in place. I have to know you'll listen to me."

He crouched down in front of her then and took her hands. "I need to know you will abide by my rules to keep you safe, and if you can't—well, I don't think I can do this— do us. I can't have a wife I can't protect. Do you understand me?" he asked harshly.

Suddenly, he stopped. The room was instantly dead quiet as Annie sat with her lips parted in surprise and Lukas came to the realization of what he had just said.

Almost in a whisper, Annie broke the silence, saying, "Wife? You don't have a wife."

Shit. Had her really said that out loud? He sat back down directly in front of her but she backed away.

"No. I don't have a wife —yet! But I want one. I want

you, Annie. But I need you to allow me to love you, protect you and even spank you. I get that that's hard to accept. I'm a hard guy. I need to know you will listen to me. I have to be in charge absolutely when your well-being is at stake." One look at Annie's face shut him up completely.

Lukas was shocked to see her face drain of color and almost just as quickly turn red. He saw her teeth clench and was even more shocked when she pushed at his chest so hard that he lost his balance and nearly fell to the floor. Annie took that opportunity to push past him and stand stiffly, hands fisted, several feet away. He reached for her, thinking she would run off in anger, but she shocked him again by holding her arms up in a stopping motion and screaming, "Stay there! Right there!" He had never seen her so incensed nor heard her speak in a voice so filled with fury.

"Let me get this straight. Are you saying that what happened with Jed was somehow *my* fault? That my lack of common sense let it happen? Because that's what it sounded like! And you say you were afraid for me? How do you think I felt? I was petrified!" When he tried to speak again, Annie's anger ramped up. "No! Just no! I'm talking now and you're going to listen. I'm in charge right now."

The wave of regret washing over Lukas was unlike anything he had ever experienced. And she wasn't finished.

"And was that your idea of a proposal? *Telling* me to be your wife, then issuing an ultimatum?"

He saw that she was truly angry and deeply hurt and it turned a knife in his heart. Suddenly, he understood that the words he had said were all wrong. He had made a big mistake and the results of that mistake were clear as the beautiful little volcano he loved erupted. Lukas had rarely been at such a loss about what to do or say.

Annie took a step forward, eyes blazing, as she said, "You say you admire me—appreciate me—find me beautiful—

even love me! Then without an ounce of tenderness or romance, you tell me you want a wife and that wife will be me, but only if I agree to let you be the boss of me always!" Now, Annie began to break down but she continued, and Lukas had the good sense to let her. "I told you I understand you want to protect me and I said I would try to follow your rules. I thought I was compromising. I even said that if you spanked me, it wouldn't be a dealbreaker but... but... it seems that's not enough for you!" Annie angrily swiped at the tears coursing down her cheeks and took a deep breath. "Right now, I'm confused and hurt and I don't even want to look at you, much less be your wife—if that's even what you meant." Lukas tried once more to speak but she screamed, "No! No! Don't talk to me. Leave me alone!"

Then she turned on her heel and ran toward the bedroom—the guest bedroom. She slammed the door and he could hear the lock click. Lukas stood by the door listening to her heartbreaking cries. God—he was an idiot! He couldn't think of a way to even begin to make things right and he sure couldn't do it now, so he sat down on the floor outside her bedroom door to wait out the storm. He hoped to hell he hadn't lost her for good but he knew it was a possibility.

Chapter 14

WHILE HE COULD HEAR her crying, Lukas sat outside the door with his head in his hands, unable to think of anything but how he had caused this. She was right. He had been an insensitive asshole and while he didn't deserve her forgiveness, he had to try.

Though he wanted to break down the door, he understood that would get him nowhere. So he waited. When it became quiet and he assumed she had cried herself to sleep, he began to try to get a handle on what had caused him to lose his mind dealing with her. She was driving him crazy—but why? He worked to honestly assess what had gone wrong. What had motivated him to say all the wrong things?

He tried to think methodically. Okay. He loved her so much that his natural dominance —which translated into protectiveness—was in high gear. If she was a different kind of woman, it might have been simpler. He would make rules for her to follow and she would stay safe. But with most women, there was no need for rules because most women didn't take the risks she did.

They were not Annie. Annie was a fearless crusader for

those whom she felt needed her. She leapt out in front of danger sometimes without thinking if she felt her cause was just and even more if someone needed protection. He identified with that. They were alike in that way. She believed that it was up to her to use her gifts of strength and intelligence to lift up and protect others. Her life as an indigenous woman working in her community had put her in risky and sometimes dangerous situations and she didn't shy away from them. On the contrary, she marched right in. He had not given her credit for the way she viewed her purpose.

Suddenly, it occurred to Lukas that his dilemma was that he wanted to be the protector of a protector. If he loved Annie as he thought he did, he would have to accept that he could only protect her up to a point. He couldn't keep her wrapped in cotton in a box away from the people she wanted to serve. But neither could he allow her to troop into danger without him. There needed to be a significant compromise. He had to convince her that he could keep her more safe than she would be on her own. Taking some basic precautions, could reduce her chances of getting hurt. Keeping her phone charged and on her at all times, calling for help and not engaging with those who might do her harm, letting him know where she was at all times—these were some things he hoped she could agree to do. If he could just get her to submit to a few important rules, he could rest a little easier. This was the agreement he would need to make with her. He understood that now, but he had not been able to articulate that to her earlier and had, instead, botched things up royally. He might not ever get a chance to work this out with her but he had to try.

Before he could explain that compromise to her, he had to come up with a plan to win her back—to make this all right. Lukas sat on the floor outside her bedroom door for a long time wracking his brain for the ideas and words that he could use so that she would listen—ones that would resonate with Annie. He would have to woo her with some serious romance, and as he thought, he got some ideas. He'd describe how he felt when he first saw her and fell in love with her, telling her that he found her to be the most beautiful and sensual woman he had ever met. He'd tell her that he could not imagine a life without her now. He would try to explain how the word 'wife' had come out naturally, as he had been thinking about her becoming his wife for a long time and that he was so sorry to have clumsily thrown it out there before preparing her for the idea of marriage. Finally, he would apologize profusely for the careless way he spoke that hurt her so much.

There was really nothing more he could do but offer sincere words of love along with a pleading apology. If she needed more time, he'd give her that. If she flat out refused, he'd have to find a way to deal with that too.

Having at least thought through a plan, he was exhausted, and convinced that there was nothing more he could do tonight, he dragged himself to bed. He knew he would have to be patient and tenacious but he'd do anything to make things up to her. Lukas finally fell into a fitful sleep.

It was still dark when Annie awoke. She had a headache and was horrified when she saw herself in the bathroom mirror. Her eyes and face were blotchy and swollen from crying and her hair was a wild mess. When she recalled the events of the night before, her heart felt heavy. Lukas had been so thoughtless and even hurtful. She had trusted him and now she was not at all convinced that he loved her. She needed time and space to consider their relationship. The idea of facing him in the morning seemed like too much.

She really wanted to be alone to think. She needed to get out of there.

Annie took two aspirin, cleaned up the best she could, got dressed in layers, and very quietly opened the door to her room. The house was silent, so she was sure Lukas was still asleep. She found her jacket and a hat, and after grabbing an apple out of the basket on the kitchen counter and stuffing her phone into a pocket, she quietly made her way out the front door.

It was not quite dawn and it was colder than she had anticipated, but when she looked up at the sky, her breath hitched. Both the moon and the sun were visible and there were still stars spread out across a sky that were an indescribable color of blue/black. The distraction briefly lifted her spirits and she took a deep breath of cool, fresh air and closed her eyes. A gust of cold wind brought her back to reality and sent a chill through her, causing her to stuff her hands into the pockets of her jacket and walk a little faster. She hadn't had a destination in mind, thinking that she just needed to clear her head, so as she walked, she lowered her eyes to the ground in front of her and began to brood. She was so angry at Lukas, but was she really angry enough to give up on him? No. She loved him. But the way he talked to her last night could not stand and she didn't know how to handle it.

She was walking along the county road that led into the very small town of Brussels. She figured it was about six o'clock in the morning now and the early time and the fact that it was a weekend explained the fact that there were no cars on the road. It really was incredibly peaceful. As she came around a bend in the road, she realized she had walked all the way to Maybelle's Diner which was open for breakfast. The diner lights looked so friendly in the hazy morning light, so Annie decided to stop in for a cup of coffee. There was only one van in the parking lot so she wouldn't have to interact with a lot of people. As she walked in, the waitress called a cheery hello and Annie told her she'd love a cup of coffee. She sat down in a booth and looked at a menu but she found she wasn't at all hungry. She had too much on her mind. Putting down the menu, her eyes went to a couple sitting in a booth along the back wall. The indigenous woman looked young—maybe even a teenager—while the man was white and quite a bit older. As she wondered at their relationship, she watched as he moved from the booth seat facing the girl to sit next to her and put his arm around her. Then he pulled her roughly to him and kissed her in a way that was inappropriate for a public place. Embarrassed, Annie looked away but not before she saw the waitress cast a worried glance their way. She also noticed the cook looking at the couple with interest. Something was not right. The hair on Annie's neck felt tingly and her danger radar was activated. She decided to order some breakfast and stay a little while. Annie got up and called to the waitress, "Could I have some pancakes and bacon? I'll just be in the bathroom a minute."

"Sure thing, sweetie," said the waitress.

Annie purposely walked past the booth where the couple was seated and tried to glance furtively at the young woman's face. She briefly made eye contact with the girl who looked frightened. The man grabbed her jaw roughly and said, "Eyes here, bitch."

Annie knew the girl was in trouble but also knew she was powerless to do anything about it. She made her way into the bathroom to consider her options. As she looked at herself in the mirror, she realized that the only option she had was to get help—and that help would have to be Lukas. She grabbed her phone and pressed his name. It rang just once before Lukas answered and with panic and anger in his voice said, "Where the hell are you, Annie? What the fuck are you doing?"

"Lukas, listen to me," she said in a hoarse whisper. "I'm in the bathroom at Maybelle's and there's a couple in the diner. I'm not sure, but I think he is holding her against her will. She's young—and indigenous. He's… he's rough with her. I don't know what to do."

Lukas' blood turned to ice and he fought to sound calm and reassuring. "You did the right thing calling, baby. I'll be right there. Keep an eye on them but don't engage. Do you hear me? Don't call attention to yourself. Everything will be okay. I'm on my way."

Just as Lukas disconnected, the waitress ran into the bathroom in a panic.

"Can you help me? That guy with the girl. He's in here every week or so with a different girl. I think he's trafficking them. They come in here, and the next day, I hear about a missing girl from Oneida or Potawatomi. What can we do?"

Annie put a hand on the waitress' shoulder and said, "I've called for help. It will be okay. Go back out there and act as normal as you can." The waitress looked frightened. "Listen to me," Annie said, holding her shoulders securely. "You can do this. Take a deep breath and do your job. It will be okay."

The waitress nodded and headed for the door, but just then, the cook came barging through.

"What the fuck are you bitches doing back here?" he snarled. He grabbed the waitress and backhanded her so hard, she fell to the floor. He glared at Annie and spitting venom said, "And you—mind your own fucking business." But then, instead of coming for her, he opened the door and yelled, "Romero, we got trouble back here!"

"Grab the squaw. I'll take both of them," called the older man. "Get them in the van—now!"

Annie fought like a wildcat but the cook was a large,

muscular Latino who was able to secure her wrists in a zip tie before she could break away. Then he picked her up over his shoulder and headed for the van, where the older man was already loading the whimpering teenager into the back. The cook threw her into the van so hard that she hit her head and saw stars. It also knocked the air out of her. When he slammed the door, it was pitch black in the windowless panel van.

By the time Annie caught her breath and was able to maneuver into a sitting position, the young woman was sobbing.

"Help is coming. Try to be brave. I'm here with you," said Annie as calmly as she could. When the girl kept crying, Annie said, "Can you tell me your name?"

"Misha. My name is Misha."

"What happened, Misha," asked Annie.

"He told me he would get me a modeling job—my dad left us and my mom needs help with money—I thought I was helping," the young girl wailed.

Just as Annie opened her mouth to try to comfort her, the van lurched forward and the girls were tossed to the floor. Then everything happened at once. Suddenly, there were sirens approaching, getting louder and louder. Did Lukas call the police? Then there was a deafening squeal of tires and a crash. The girls were thrown savagely against the back door. Annie was able to protect her head but Misha was knocked unconscious. The sirens were just outside the van now and Annie heard men's voices yelling. Annie began calling desperately for help, and within minutes, the back doors of the van were yanked open. There was Lukas whose eyes wildly searched the dark interior for Annie.

"Thank God," Lukas said as he reached for her.

"Lukas! I'm okay. I'm okay, but Misha needs help. She hit

her head!" Annie said as she let herself cry now that the Lukas was here for her.

"Come with me," he said, stepping out of the van and picking her up in his arms as a medic raced past him to get to Misha. For a moment, Lukas was so overcome with relief and gratitude he couldn't move, but when Annie snuggled her face into his neck, he pressed a kiss to her temple and made his way to the ambulance to get her checked out. He grabbed his pocket knife to cut the tie holding her wrists and Annie threw her arms around his neck.

"Jesus Christ, Annie, are you sure you're okay?" Lukas asked with emotion clogging his throat.

She looked up at him through tears, saying, "You came! You're here! I didn't know if you still loved me!" Annie cried, tightening her hold on him.

Her words were like a knife in his heart. "Baby, baby, let me see you," he said as he grabbed her face and then ran his hands over every part of her, assuring himself she was whole. "Don't you ever think I don't love you. You own my heart, little girl,"

Lukas must have looked a wreck—he knew his heart was ready to beat out of his chest—because the medic said, "Hey, buddy, take some deep breaths and try to calm down some. Are you okay?"

He wasn't okay, but he guessed life with Annie was always going to be punctuated with moments of terror and that he would have to accept that. But he would do all he could to persuade her to accept his guidance and protection to reduce those moments. They were going to have a serious talk.

Chapter 15

"WE BELIEVE this guy is part of a human trafficking ring that has been picking off young indigenous women one by one around here consistently for weeks. The cook was a paid accomplice," the young detective from the tribal police told them as he finished taking their statements. "We'll find out exactly how this all went down, but I know we owe you a debt of gratitude," he said, looking at Lukas and Annie. Then he stood and gave them each his card and said, "Call me if you think of anything else. And thanks."

Misha and her mother were being taken to a shelter for girls and women who had been trafficked or experienced trauma related to it. They would stay there to heal for a couple of weeks and then Annie had promised that she and Lukas would help them with living arrangements and support.

Lukas shook the young man's hand and Annie smiled and then couldn't help a huge yawn.

"Let's get you home," said Lukas, guiding her to his truck and lifting her in.

Thankfully, the trip home was just a few minutes because

the silence between them was uncomfortable. Lukas and Annie had so much to figure out.

As soon as she walked in the door, Annie said, "I need to take a shower," and she started to turn to walk down the hall. But Lukas turned her to face him.

"Hey, after your shower, I'd like you to eat and then maybe go back to bed for a while. You're exhausted," Lukas said gently, unsure if she was still carrying last night's anger.

When she compliantly agreed, it actually worried him some but he kissed her on the forehead and said, "I'll make those waffles you like, yeah?"

Annie nodded and smiled weakly then turned away.

Lukas wondered what was keeping Annie. He had heard the shower go off a while ago. He had made waffles and set them under the warming lights to wait. Finally, he went looking for her. When he didn't find her in the bathroom or in the bedroom where she had slept, he was alarmed. Had she taken off again? He was just about to call out her name when he decided to look in his room. He was flooded with relief when he saw Annie sound asleep on his bed where she must have crashed after her shower. He took the opportunity to take in her sleeping form. Her body was lush and inviting, and he felt his cock grow hard just at the sight of her lying there on her tummy with one leg drawn up. She had donned one of his long-sleeved thermal shirts and while it was way too big, her position allowed him to see her perfect bottom peeking out. The black gleaming waves of her freshly washed hair fanned out over the pillow and around her face. He wanted her with every fiber of his being but knew he couldn't act on that until they established a direction for their future. Frustrated, he cursed a blue streak in his head, ran a hand through his hair, and left her there to rest.

He grabbed a pack of cigarettes from his refrigerator and stormed out the door to stand on the deck. He lit up, took a satisfying drag and let the sun, which was pleasantly warming up the day, soothe him and let him think clearly. He knew he was completely in love with Annie and wanted her with him always—to marry her. The seeds of a plan began in his head and started to grow. After a little while, he had an idea of how to proceed and was anxious to try it out.

As if the universe perceived his resolve, he heard a noise behind him, and there, standing in a ray of sunlight, was Annie. Her long, golden legs extended down from his shirt that reached her thighs. She stood demurely on bare feet, one leg crossed in front of the other and her arms wrapped around herself. The sun reflected blindingly off her titian hair and she was holding her bottom lip in her teeth. When she raised her dark eyes to him, he had to swallow his emotions down before he could hold out his arms and say, "Come here, baby."

Lukas grabbed a sun-warmed throw from a deck chair, wrapped it around her and pulled her into his arms.

"Christ, Annie. You are so goddamned beautiful," he said in his deep, gravelly voice. She smiled then—a big, genuine, smile that he hoped contained forgiveness.

"I'm so sorry I hurt your feelings last night, baby. I was an idiot. I didn't make any sense. Will you let me try again?"

She nodded, still smiling, and put her arms around his neck. He picked her up and sat her on one of the high deck chairs and stood between her open legs. He held her face in his hands and Annie was sure she saw his heart in his eyes.

He swallowed hard then and began. "Falling in love with you has been the most wonderful yet frightening thing I've ever done. You know I'm used to being in charge—calling the shots—dominating the action," he said seriously.

"You've made that crystal clear, Lukas," she said, giving him no indication of her mood. But he continued. It was now or never.

"Then you also know that my need to protect you and keep you safe is part of me."

"That's clear also, Lukas," she said.

"I love everything about you, Annie, just the way you are. I respect and admire you." He paused for a moment before continuing. "But I can't change. I can't be someone else in order to keep you."

She surprised him by saying, "I understand, Lukas."

"You do?" he asked, his eyes growing wide.

"I do, and let me tell you some things," she said, putting her hands against his chest. "I also love everything about you. But I've been independent for a long time now and compliant is not a word anyone would use to describe me."

"You've made that crystal clear, Annie," he said, the corners of his mouth turning up slightly.

"And I don't think I can change my stripes, either," she continued. "But you're a remarkable man and I understand now that the part of me that wants you to be happy is the same part that will allow you to be in charge when you need to. And—true confession—when you make rules and go all bossy on me, it somehow seems right." She was blushing now but went on. "I have somehow come to understand—and appreciate—that your actions are born of love. And even though it sometimes drives me crazy and sometimes makes me angry, I still want you—always. I'm willing to accept all of you, even spankings, if you are willing to accept all of me —even risk taking." As she spoke, her eyes began to fill with tears and by the time she was finished, she couldn't help make a small sobbing sound.

"Baby, I love you," he said as he slanted his lips over hers and kissed her deeply—kissed her like he never wanted to let her go. She kissed him back, and as she did, she shrugged off the blanket and wrapped her legs around him. As a cool breeze surrounded them, he put his hands under her bottom and lifted her—with lips still locked—to carry her inside. She squealed as he gently sat her on the large chair in front of the fire. She began to giggle, but before she realized what was happening, she saw that Lukas was down on one knee in front of her and was holding a small velvet box that he had produced seemingly out of thin air. Annie's hands flew to her face as her mouth made a perfect "O".

"Annie Summerhill, I am begging you to be my wife, not telling you—no ultimatums—just pure begging," he said, opening the box to reveal an exquisite art deco engagement ring. There were three diamonds set in yellow gold that had a lovely patina indicating it had been worn with love for many years. "This ring was my grandmother's and my mother's, but I will not be offended if you'd like to get a new one. I've kept this ring here since my mother died and I thought maybe now would be a good time to see if it would help me seal the deal. Let's see if it worked." He took her hand and looked into her eyes. "Will you marry me, Annie?"

Now, she was full-out crying, but she managed to say, "Yes! Yes! Yes! I will marry you," and as Lukas took her hand to slip the ring on her finger, she said, "and the ring. I love it. It means so much. It's beautiful!"

Annie began to plant butterfly kisses all over his face until he put his hand on the back of her neck and guided her into a passionate kiss that left her breathless. Lukas stood with her then and when she looked up at him, he had a strange look on his face.

"Is there something wrong?" she asked.

"No, baby. Everything is right, and to keep it that way, I

need to begin how I mean to go on." And with that, he bent down and lifted Annie over his shoulder.

"What are you doing?" she screeched as he headed toward his bedroom, sat on the bed and stood her in front of him between his legs. When he grabbed her wrists, she again asked in a panic, "What are you doing, Lukas?"

With a lowered chin and a furrowed brow, he said, "Sneaking out of here this morning was foolish and turned out to be downright dangerous. You could have been hurt badly or worse."

"But, Lukas—" she sputtered.

"No. I've watched you put yourself in risky situations more than a few times since we met and that is going to stop —now!" he said sternly. Lukas almost laughed when he saw the reality of the situation dawn on Annie.

"You mean you're going to… going to…"

"Spank you. Yup. I'm going to light a fire on that bottom that you won't soon forget. Hopefully, you'll remember this before you race off without thinking again," he said, dragging her over one of his huge thighs, using his other leg to secure both of hers. "Running off this morning was beyond foolish. You were almost kidnapped!"

"But, Lukas," she cried desperately, "you can't spank me today—not now—this is our engagement day!"

"No better time, baby," he said as he secured her arms to the small of her back.

Annie immediately began to scream and struggle with everything she had, but she was no match for Lukas and because she conveniently had no panties on, her bare bottom was immediately perched vulnerably up in the air, ready for his first smacks. And there was no warm up. Lukas spanked hard from the beginning. He had hoped to teach Annie the pleasures of a playful good girl spanking before he had to resort to the real thing, but this was how it turned out.

There'd be plenty of time for play later. For now, she needed a hard lesson and he hoped a sore bottom would be a deterrent for future thoughtless behavior.

Annie was shocked at how much the spanking hurt. She truly felt he was setting her bottom on fire. And she was angry—so angry that she called him every profane word she had ever heard—but when that seemed to make things worse, she opted for begging him to stop. "Please, Lukas, stop! Stop!

"Spankings stop when I think you've learned your lesson, baby, and we're not there yet," he said, moving his aim down to her thighs, which had her screaming anew.

Annie then began to make promises. "I'll never do it again. I'll listen to you. I'll be good—I swear!"

He was making headway and that was good because her stubborn streak had caused him to turn her bottom bright red and even purple in spots. Finally, she went limp over his lap, and as she lay there bawling, he stopped. She tried to get up, but he held her there, waiting for her to calm a bit. Then he stood her up, drew her onto his lap and grabbed some tissues to wipe her face.

Annie winced when he put his hand on her very hot bottom to pull her close but she didn't try to get away. In fact, she put her free arm around his neck, buried her face in his chest and cried, "I'm sorry, Lukas. I'm sorry." He rocked her then, making shushing sounds until her crying was reduced to sniffles and hiccups.

Just then, Annie's stomach growled—loudly.

"Time to get you something to eat, baby girl. I've got waffles waiting for you. Let's go," he said, lifting her off his lap.

Annie stood, folded her arms and said petulantly, "I'm not hungry. You go eat by yourself."

Lukas laughed as he grabbed her to stand between his

legs again, which had her ineffectively pulling away. "Hold up, baby. Listen to me," he said as he lifted her chin to look at him. "That spanking means you're forgiven—we can start new—start over. But if you think you can drag this out or make me feel guilty by pouting or throwing a tantrum, it won't work. In fact, I'm likely to put you right back over my knee and refresh that sting. Do you hear me?"

Annie glared at him until he moved to tip her over his knee again when she said, "I hear you. I hear you. I won't pout."

"Good girl," he said, lifting her to kiss her forehead.

"But, Lukas?"

"What is it, baby?"

"Can I get dressed before I eat?"

"No. I think you're more likely to remember this lesson if you spend some time sitting on a bare bottom, so how about you get some slippers for your feet but then you come and eat just like you are?"

Knowing she had no choice, Annie got some socks from his dresser. Lukas stood to go to the kitchen as Annie yanked on the socks and said under her breath, "There are a lot of spanking rules, I guess."

"Yes, there are, baby, and you'd do well to remember them," called Lukas, heading out the bedroom door. Safely out of his view, Annie stamped her foot and stuck her tongue out in the direction Lukas had gone. Then she took a deep breath and followed him to breakfast.

As she came into the kitchen, Lukas had just answered his phone and she could tell he was talking to Dax. This must mean he and Dyani were home from their honeymoon. Annie couldn't wait to see Dyani again.

Lukas moved around the kitchen, still talking to Dax, and put a plate with waffles and strawberry syrup on the table indicating Annie should sit. She ignored him, poured herself some orange juice and then picked up her plate to move it to the island where she planned to stand while eating. Her bottom was way too sore to sit on the hard wooden chair. Lukas saw what she did and grabbed her plate to put it back on the table. Then—still carrying on a conversation with Dax—he pulled out her chair, pointed to it firmly and glared at her until she begrudgingly sat down with an attitude—and a wince. He stood next to her chair until she began to eat while he concluded his talk with Dax.

"Yeah, that would be great. I know the girls are dying to see each other and we can talk about the legal center pilot." Pause. "Sure. We can be there around noon tomorrow." Pause. "Thanks, Dax. See you later."

As soon as he finished, Annie popped excitedly out of her chair and grabbed Lukas' forearms, almost making him drop his plate. "We're going to see Dax and Dyani? Tomorrow? I can't wait!" she said, nearly vibrating.

"They've invited us for brunch tomorrow morning," he said, looking down into her happy face and deciding not to scold her. "Now, please eat as much of that breakfast as you can. I'm tired of hearing your growly tummy complain about being empty."

Annie flashed a grin at him and said, "Okay, Daddy," as she sat down obediently and gingerly. He kissed the top of her head and joined her at the table.

Chapter 16

DYANI HADN'T HAD a chance to talk to Annie since before the frightening break-in at the center about ten days ago. She knew Annie was okay, but she and Lukas had been tied up getting the young woman and her son safe and settled. She would be happy to see—and hug—Annie again and she wanted to hear all the details about the incident. Dax knew she was anxious to see her friend again and it was so thoughtful of him to call Lukas to come to brunch on Sunday. She knew Dax was very interested in the legal center Lukas was hoping to set up at Oneida and wanted to see how he could help. Once again, Dyani reflected on what a miracle it was that Dax came into her life. She was head-over-heels in love with him.

They were home now at Cave Point, which Dyani was just beginning to think of as "theirs". It was a spectacular home made even more wonderful with the addition of a fully equipped and stocked ceramic studio for Dyani. Dax had surprised her with that lavish gift as a celebration of their engagement. It was still hard for her to believe that he had arranged for the studio to be set up and nearly completed as a surprise when they had been out of town on a getaway last summer.

After their beautiful wedding last month at Oneida Farm, Dyani and Dax had taken a small honeymoon to their home on Washington Island. Dax had wanted to spend a month in Hawaii but Dyani persuaded him to put that off until midwinter. Their week had been nearly perfect. The serene peace and quiet of life in a place where no cars were allowed and where very few people lived year-round was the nest for their relationship to grow and flourish. They talked for hours as they took long walks all over the island. They cooked together and enjoyed leisurely meals or just sat and read in cozy, sunlit rooms. And they made love.

Dax had been happy to discover Dyani's innate, if not naïve, sensuality and her eagerness to learn about its joys. She followed his lead and seemed to be eager to explore every suggestion he made. They made love in every position and in every room of the sprawling ranch. Clothes became inconvenient and he finally allowed her to wear only his t-shirts so he would have access to her at all times and she was always wet and ready for him. The Daddy/little girl dynamic Dax had hoped for had become a foundation they both found natural and it had been in full play as they reveled in the luxurious privacy of their getaway. Dax's dominance aroused her and when she called him 'Daddy', he couldn't resist her. During this 'honeymoon' week, he had given her several good girl spankings and experimented with bondage which they both found highly erotic. There had been no call for him to administer any real spankings or other punishments as it was nearly impossible for her to get into trouble there, but he would not have hesitated because he knew that even standing in a corner with a sore bottom on display, or being required to wear a naughty girl plug for the day made her body react with need and want. Dax's stamina never wavered and the entire week had passed in a lust-filled haze. It was difficult to come home to a regular routine so he had insisted they go back to normal life slowly, still allowing plenty of time for each other. Dyani's reunion with Annie would be the first time since the wedding she had interacted with anyone but him, but he knew she needed her friend. And Dax had wanted to talk to Lukas about his future plans at the Farm.

For now, he heard Dyani turn off the shower as he stood —bare-chested and barefoot— in the kitchen pouring a fresh cup of coffee. He heard her pad through the great room to the kitchen, and when he turned so their eyes met, he saw her pupils go dark as her breath hitched. He recognized that look and it made him feel like a god. He saw that she had dressed in a soft shirt of her own and yoga pants and he saw a chance for play.

"What are you wearing, little girl?" he asked, pushing himself away from the counter to rise to his full overpowering height in front of her. Dyani looked down and immediately brought her hand to her mouth, indicating that she had genuinely forgotten his orders about only wearing his shirts. He moved toward her like a panther stalking his prey. "What did I tell you about dressing when we're at home?" She took a step back, but in one lightning swift movement, she found herself being held under his arm and across his hip so that her bottom was in a perfect position for a smack.

"Answer me, Dyani. What did I tell you about getting dressed?" he said as he put two fingers in the waistband of her pants and lowered them very slowly down over her perfect ass. The morning sun was pouring in, highlighting her flawless skin. Dax loved the color of Dyani's skin, which was a caramel gold but light enough to see his handprint bloom as he brought his hand down in a meaningful spank.

"Ow! Daddy, please! You told me I could only wear your

shirts, but I didn't know that rule was for here at home too. I'm sorry," Dyani said in a tone that was only mildly pleading as she was pretty sure he wasn't really angry. She squirmed and tried to escape, but he edged her pants down to the middle of her thighs, increasing the feeling of vulnerability that aroused her.

His cock hardened to steel as she called him Daddy and as he thought about turning her little bottom bright pink.

"You didn't know, huh? Well, I'm going to help you remember that I'm in charge of lifting limits and I haven't given you permission to wear anything but my shirts," he said, picking her up under his arm and walking with her.

"Okay. But I'm sorry, Daddy," she said.

"Not as sorry as you will be," he said as he moved to the massive sectional in the great room, matching a swat with nearly every step. He sat on the back of the large piece and drew her over one huge leg. He refreshed his handprint with a slap and moved two fingers into her folds to find her clit ready for him—she was wet with need. Dyani was not resisting or trying to escape his grip but, instead, pushed her sweet, pink bottom up, wanting more.

Dax reached down and pulled her pants completely off, saying, "This naughty bottom is going to stay bare for the rest of the day. But first, you're getting a spanking." He secured her legs with one of his own and began a steady rhythm of swats that caused just enough of a sting to make Dyani worry that this was indeed a punishment. Her bottom was just becoming uncomfortably hot when he stopped, stood with her, and carried her on his hip to the bedroom. She wrapped her legs around his waist and hung on to him, burying her face in his neck. Dax held her with his large hand over her bottom and slipped a finger inside, making her gasp as he asked, "Are you going to be a good girl now?"

"Oh, Daddy, I don't know if I can," she said in a little girl voice.

He pinched her clit, making her cry out, and said in a voice that was deep and grumbly, "Do you know the expression 'don't poke the bear?'" She bit her lip and nodded as he put her down next to his expansive bed. "Well, you're poking the bear right now—and that's dangerous."

"But, Daddy, I'm crazy about the bear and I-I trust him," she said coyly, putting her hands up to his chest.

He smiled but then turned her and, with a tremendous swat to her already warm backside, said, "Get your ass in that bed—now!" As she scrambled to obey, he added, "And spread those legs—wide."

The dominant tone in his voice shot straight to Dyani's core—as it always did—keeping her quiet and turning her on. She watched him shed his pants, crawl on the bed, and rise up over her on his knees looking for all the world like a warrior claiming victory. His naked body looked so hot, she thought she might ignite. He grabbed her wrists in one hand and held them above her head while he caressed one breast, roughly pinching her nipple. She moaned into his mouth as he leaned down in an all-possessing kiss that caused electricity to course through her from head to toe. After giving her other breast the same attention, leaving her nipples as hard as pebbles, he let go of her wrists but said, "Don't move those hands. Keep them up there, or you'll get more than a play spanking, hear?"

He chuckled as she stretched her arms farther above her head in an effort to demonstrate compliance, but when he slid his giant hands down her ribs to span her narrow waist and dragged his rough chin down along the skin from her breasts to her tummy, she began to vibrate with need. Unable to think clearly, she lowered her hands to grab his head, to which he immediately responded by grasping her hip, turning her slightly to give her half a dozen smacks that were much harder than the previous ones. Her breath caught and she cried out, "Ow! Ow! Oh, please, Daddy, stop. I'll be good."

She was beyond ready for him and spread her legs as far as she could as he thrust into her, making her wonder again if she really could accommodate his girth. But very soon, as he began to drive powerfully deep within her, she began to match his rhythm. She could feel her tightness wrapped around him as she felt her orgasm beginning to unfurl and it took everything she had, to keep her hands in place to obey him.

As she approached her climax and they were both moaning with pleasure, he put his lips near her ear and said, "Damn right, you'll be a good little girl, or this Daddy will get his paddle and add some welts to that sore bottom."

His words alone would have pushed her over the edge, but when he reached behind her to press his thumb into her small rosebud, the pain and pleasure of that action had her writhing helplessly until she absolutely exploded, screaming out his name. She was no longer able to keep her arms above her head but wrapped them around him and covered him with kisses. Dax stiffened then and, with a roar, spilled his seed as she continued to milk his cock. She cried out, begging him not to stop and reminding him that she loved him, even as her legs strained to stay open and her voice began to become hoarse.

So that he was not trapping her under his body, Dax rolled to his side, taking her with him to wait for their breathing to stop thundering in their ears and their hearts to stop racing. Dyani cuddled her face into his neck, and even after he gently pulled out, she moved in so close that there was no space between their bodies. When he began to speak,

Dyani was reminded of how she adored the vibrating sound of his deep voice as she lay with her face on his chest.

When he spoke, it was with deep emotion. "You know, baby, I have never understood addictions—until now. I'm addicted to you. I can't get enough, can't tear myself away. I don't ever want you more than an arm's length from me and I want unfettered access to every part of your perfect body all the time. Christ, little girl, what have you done to me?"

He kissed the top of her head tenderly while she battled with the lump in her throat and the tears threatening to spill. Finally, she took a deep breath, began to curl her finger in the light patch of hair on his chest and said, "I'll always be right here for you—whenever you want. You've trapped me, Dax." Then thinking better of those words, she rolled on top of him, took his face in her hands and said, "No. Not trapped. You've set me free. Free to need you—free to love you—free to be safe with you. I love you, Dax Dumont, every bossy inch of you."

"And I love you, baby girl," he said as he continued to hold her tightly until he heard her breathing evenly in sleep.

The fact that he wanted her again—immediately—convinced him that the word 'addiction' was more than appropriate.

Chapter 17

LUKAS WATCHED Annie put together a dried flower arrangement to take when they visited her friend Dyani and her husband later in the morning. Annie's general demeanor was usually reserved and quiet, yet watching her get ready to visit Dyani when she hadn't seen her in a while was like watching a child anticipating a birthday. She was much more animated than usual, talking a mile a minute. After she finished the flowers, Annie asked repeatedly if it was time to go yet. Her behavior was uncharacteristically child-like for her and Lukas had to smile as he told her to settle down if she wanted to sit comfortably on the way to Cave Point.

As they pulled up the long, tree-lined drive to Dax and Dyani's spectacular home, Annie saw Dyani sitting bundled up on the veranda, clearly waiting for them. Annie's eyes filled with tears, even as her face lit up at the sight of her friend who descended the stairs with her arms open. Annie all but ran into them. The young women held each other with such affection that both Dax and Lukas were struck with the emotion of the moment. The girls briefly said hello to each of the men, but then Annie handed Dyani her gift, looped her arm around her waist, and the two walked toward the house—heads bent together in catch-up conversation.

Lukas turned to Dax and said with a smile, "We might as well not even be here, huh?"

Dax watched his woman indulgently and said, "Come on in, Lukas, I want to hear all about what you've been planning."

The men had just walked in the door when delighted screams and laughter burst from the kitchen. Annie had been arranging the fall flowers in a basket when Dyani spotted her engagement ring, and by the time Dax and Lukas arrived, the girls were squealing, hugging and jumping up and down.

"Dax! They're engaged! Lukas and Annie are getting married! Isn't it wonderful?" Dyani said, her face beaming as she held Annie's hand up to show off the ring. "I'm so happy for you both!"

Dax clapped Lukas on the back and said, "Congratulations, both of you." And then he took Annie's hand and pecked her on the cheek. "It seems we have a lot to talk about and celebrate today. Why don't you get comfortable and let me get you something to eat." Then to Dyani, he said, "Can you find that champagne I keep for special events? "

"Oh," Dyani said with excitement, "I'll make mimosas!"

The couples spent the entire afternoon talking. As Annie talked about the circumstances of the incidents with Laney and Thomas and then with Misha at the diner, Dax noticed the possessive and protective way Lukas watched Annie and the way his large body sat surrounding her small one. He could only imagine how out of his mind he would be if

Dyani had been in either of those situations. As they talked, it became clear to Dax and Dyani that Lukas was in charge and had set some ground rules he expected Annie to follow. It was also clear that she had already learned the conse- quences of not submitting to Lukas' direction. Dyani remem- bered how persistent Lukas had been in trying to get Annie's attention and how she had resisted him mightily. That seemed to be resolved now and Annie seemed much more compliant. Whatever had finally brought them together, Dyani was thrilled for her dear friend, who seemed quite in love. She couldn't wait to get Annie alone to hear all about it.

When the topic turned to the legal center pilot plan, Dyani was not really surprised that Lukas and Annie had decided it would be best if they worked together, bringing different perspectives and talents to the project. They had already proven themselves a well-suited team who worked in almost a symbiotic way. The work they had done in the last couple of weeks with indigenous women in trouble had proven that. Dyani and Dax both thought the proposal for the legal center was remarkable and they were deeply impressed.

As they finished their coffee, still seated at the table, and Lukas further explained the ways in which their clients could be helped, something clicked in Dyani's head and she said, "I know this may not be on your radar, but I was wondering if you have a name for this new entity you're putting together. Will it just be called Oneida Legal Center or Women's Resource Center? Or were you thinking something else?"

"You know, we hadn't thought about that at all yet, Dyani. Maybe we should. Do you have any ideas?" asked Annie.

Dyani blushed a little and peeped up at Dax from under her lashes. "Well, I just got an idea."

Finding her impossibly adorable, Dax grabbed Dyani's

wrist and pulled her to sit on his lap. He kissed her temple and asked, "What's your idea, baby?"

Dyani put an arm around Dax's neck and looked at Annie. "Well, the designs I've been most recently working on with my pottery are various perspectives of the sun. I'd been thinking about making a set of mugs or bowls to honor both the winter and summer solstice. I remembered that my grandparents put a lot of stock in acknowledging each solstice. They saw the winter one as a time of rebirth as we get ready to move into the light after the longest night of the year and the summer solstice as a celebration of light finally returned. They had many stories to tell, and as kids, we always made crafts that had to do with the sun. My grandma always said that the winter solstice brought the hope of more light, longer days and warmth—things we all want and need —things we all need to be assured of."

There were tears in Annie's eyes as she moved to crouch down in front of Dyani to take her hands and say, "The Solstice Center. Are you thinking The Solstice Center?" asked Annie as Dyani nodded while tears also filled her eyes.

"It will be a place of rebirth, hope, new beginnings and light. Oh, Dyani! It's so perfect," she said as both girls stood and hugged. "Really, it's a beautiful name. I love it."

It wasn't the first time that Dax and Lukas had observed the deep bond shared by their women and were wise enough to let them have their time.

Finally, Annie turned to Lukas, who smiled and said, "I agree that it's perfect. Solstice Center, it is."

Then as Lukas began to get down into the detailed weeds of how the legal center would work, Dax suggested they go to his office to talk finances and Annie asked Dyani to take her to the studio to see her 'sun' and 'solstice' designs.

After Dyani shared the incredible designs she was working on, the young women sat on a comfy, overstuffed sofa with cups of herbal tea, in front of the welcoming fireplace. Dax had designed a studio for Dyani that was part studio and part living space, with a kitchenette, lounging area and hearth. It seemed like the perfect place and time for Annie to share everything about how she had struggled to open herself to the kind of man Lukas was. She told Dyani all about his need to keep her safe and her reluctance to succumb to his rules and general take-charge nature.

Dyani listened carefully, not offering opinions, but rather showing empathy for Annie's dilemma. By the time she finally told Dyani that they had reached a compromise with Annie understanding that she had to heed his rules and advice for her own safety or suffer the consequences that might include spanking, Annie was full-on blushing.

But Dyani was smiling kindly when she said, "You love him, yes?"

"Yes," said Annie. "And it's not just that, Dyani. I… well, I sometimes find his dominant manner arousing." She covered her face with her hands when she continued, saying, "And sometimes I'm even turned on by a spanking. Oh my God. What is wrong with me?"

Dyani held her friend's hand and again explained that nothing was 'wrong' with her. She told Annie how the Daddy/little girl dynamic worked for her and Dax. "It's a part of 'us' that I love—well, I don't love a punishment spanking— but I understand it, and when I call him Daddy, we both feel we are in the right space."

"I'm still processing all of this," said Annie, squeezing her hand. "But thank you, you're a good friend."

Annie moved closer to Dyani and put her arm around her, feeling so lucky to have such a good friend. They sat there in silence for a while with Dyani's head on her shoulder, and soon she realized that Dyani had fallen asleep.

By the time it began to get dark and the men came to the

studio looking for them, both young women were dozing together, making a touching picture of friendship. They quietly watched their women for a little while when Dax said, "You know, I feel like I've died and gone to Heaven sometimes."

Lukas patted him on the shoulder and said, "I hear you, man. I hear you."

The men shook hands then with Dax reminding Lukas, "This plan you've got could be a gamechanger for the Oneida—especially the women—and I'm behind you all the way. Let me know where you want to start and I'll help you make it happen."

"Thanks, Dax. I'll be in touch." And with that, he roused Annie enough to pick her up and get her out to the truck to make their way home.

Chapter 18

THE NEXT TWO weeks were filled with several life changing events for Lukas and Annie. Both of them were juggling the difficulties—and strong emotions—that accompany life transitions.

Annie worked with Jason to get Issi up to speed to take over the management at the community center. It was November, and the schedule at the center would wind down for a few months. Jason hired one of the volunteers who had served there more than a dozen years to assist Issi, and Annie would be nearby after the new legal center was built. Annie would miss the job she had loved but had confidence in Issi's ability and high hopes for the future. After a day of getting Issi up to speed with the current activities, she seemed ready enough, so Annie could work on the many issues competing for her time.

First, there was the matter of moving in with Lukas. After their day with Dax and Dyani, Lukas was adamant that she live with him now that they were engaged. He wanted to hold her every night and keep her safe every day. The condo in Green Bay that he used when projects kept him in the city was already furnished and ready, so after moving a few things from his house in Brussels, he was all set. For now, they'd use his homestead for weekends when they could. Annie had been renting her house from the Oneida and it had been decided that the fledgling nonprofit would purchase it and transform it into a secure domestic abuse shelter for women and children. Annie's life was simple and she had very little to move. The ranch hands from the Farm were able to get all of her things into Lukas' condo in less than a day.

These changes would have been a lot on their own, but at breakfast one day, after living in his condo for just a couple of days, Lukas brought up plans to get married. He asked her what she was thinking about it.

She looked up at him, surprised. "I haven't been thinking about it." Then realizing how that sounded, she jumped down from the stool at the kitchen island, went to him and put her hands on his chest. "You know I want to marry you, to be your wife, but... but there's been a lot going on in my life—our lives—lately," she said. "I'm feeling a little over-whelmed." He looked at her seriously but allowed her to continue. "Planning a wedding and reception is a lot of work, and I just don't think I can do that along with every-thing else we're trying to get accomplished." She looked up at him and asked pleadingly, "Could we wait until next summer?"

Lukas suddenly looked angry. "Next summer? No," he almost roared. "Absolutely not." Then realizing he may have been too harsh when her eyes went wide, he picked her up to place her on the kitchen island and took her face in his hands. "Baby, listen. I want to be married—sooner, rather than later."

She put her hands up to grasp his wrists and, with tears in her eyes, said, "I want to marry you too, Lukas, but a new home—new job—new fiancé—it's a lot. The idea of planning a wedding is just too much. I'm sorry to disappoint you." Tears escaped down her cheeks, but Lukas wiped them away with his thumbs and kissed her forehead.

"You're not disappointing me, baby. There *is* a lot going on." He paused for a moment then— as if steeling himself— asked, "What do you think about going to the courthouse and getting married, like this week, then we could take all the time we want planning a wedding and reception. We could do it next summer or fall or whenever you like."

She sniffled and said, "You mean like Dax and Dyani did?"

"Yeah," he said. "Just like that. You know things worked out perfectly for them. What do you say?"

Annie looked up at him with those piercing dark eyes for what seemed to be a long time before saying, "Okay, Lukas. When?"

Annie had never seen a bigger smile on his face as he picked her up and spun her around.

Excitedly, he said, "I'll make some calls. Maybe we could do it this Friday. That gives us a few days and—"

"But Dyani has to be there. I won't do it without Dax and Dynai," she interrupted.

"Right. Do you want to call them? I'll get the private dining room at White Gull to eat dinner after. Sound good?"

Annie was smiling then as she threw her arms around Lukas' shoulders and kissed him lightly on the lips. He accepted that invitation and responded with a soul-searing kiss that had her whimpering. Then, with her breathless and giggling, he picked her up and carried her to the bedroom where they sealed the deal with tender lovemaking.

Dyani was thrilled with the news of a courthouse wedding and the girls immediately began to talk about what to wear. Annie thought she would just wear a dress she had and used before for parties, but Dyani talked her into a shopping trip for a new and special dress.

Dax drove Dyani down to Green Bay so they could shop. He had work to do with Lukas so they would hole up at the condo until the girls were finished shopping. The couples planned to meet at the end of the day at Lukas' favorite Green Bay tavern, the Black Saddle, famous for its pulled pork sandwiches. As Annie grabbed her coat and her keys, Lukas tamped down the anxiety he felt when she was out on her own and resisted listing off rules for her to follow. He didn't want to dim her excitement. She knew what he expected and so did Dyani, for that matter. They also understood the consequences, so both girls got warnings to be good and headed out, happily chattering.

Annie had never been to the boutique known as Twist—only heard about it—and it definitely lived up to its reputation as must-see. It wasn't just a clothing store, but rather an experience. The building was five thousand square feet filled with an almost overwhelming amount of artfully arranged displays of sweaters, dresses, jackets, jeans, boots and shoes, and the store vibrated with dance music. Even the dressing rooms were amazing. They were large enough to host a group of friends comfortably on overstuffed loveseats. The walls were covered in floor to ceiling mirrors and the lighting was soft and flattering. Refreshments from sparkling water to white wine were available, making the shopping experience more of a party. The sales associates were friendly but not pushy, and when they heard that Annie needed a dress for her casual wedding, they were so excited, they began bringing her armfuls of beautiful styles and colors. Annie and Dyani were having a ball and, finally, after trying on dozens of dresses, decided on an elegant gray-green sweater dress in the softest knit Annie had ever known. The color highlighted her skin tone and raven hair and the dress flattered her form but was neither too tight nor too short to be inappropriate. The dress left her shoulders bare, which was just sexy enough. Dyani found some gray suede boots with heels just high enough to enhance Annie's long legs, and when she stepped out of the dressing room to give a twirl for everyone in the store, her long, loose hair fanned around her, drawing a round of applause and tears from Dyani. Annie didn't think she had ever felt more beautiful and hoped Lukas would like it as much as she did.

It was about five thirty and just getting dark when Dyani called Dax, who told her they would meet them at the Black Saddle in about forty-five minutes for dinner.

The girls had found some seats near the end of the bar to wait and ordered glasses of wine when a bartender suggested they put in their name in if they planned on eating any time soon. He explained that the unusually large crowd was from the first day of a hunting and camping show at the nearby Resch Center. That also explained the high percentage of men in attendance.

A few men tried their hands at getting the attention of the friends, but Annie and Dyani rebuffed them repeatedly. One large, rugged-looking guy wouldn't take 'no' for an answer, and after having been turned down by both girls, came to stand again next to Annie just as the bartender was taking her name for a table.

"Oh," said Annie, loud enough to be heard. "Can you put the table under my fiancé's name? That's Lukas Mattson. He'll be here soon," she said, picking up her wine glass and bringing it to her lips with her left hand. Her ring glittered as it reflected the lights above the bar. She felt, rather than saw, the lumberjack turn and walk away. Annie turned to Dyani with a look of satisfaction and then noticed a tall, leggy blonde sitting a couple of stools away. Their eyes met briefly but then the blonde brazenly looked her over—from head to toe—and the look was not friendly. Annie looked away then, giving Dyani her full attention as they relived their enjoyable day.

After about half an hour, Annie excused herself to go to the restroom which was located down a hall in the back of the bar. Though the building was historic—exposed brick walls and original windows—the lighting was new as was all the plumbing and fixtures.

When Annie came out of the stall, there stood the blonde she had noticed earlier. Her arms were crossed and she was leaning against the towel dispenser, blocking its use. Annie noticed that the woman, though pretty, wore an abundance of make-up. That, combined with her short, black leather skirt, tight, low-cut top, and very high heels made her look cheap and tough.

When Annie moved to grab a paper towel, the woman didn't move but said with a sneer, "You don't seem his type."

Confused, Annie said, "Pardon me?"

"Lukas. You're his "fiancée" now?" she said, making air quotes. "What a joke. He asked me to marry him once too, and God knows how many other women he's led down that path. It's a line he uses to get them in bed. He's been with every slut in Green Bay," she said, straightening and standing a few inches taller than Annie. "I even hear he has some kids scattered around up here."

All color had drained from Annie's face. She didn't want to believe anything this woman was saying, but it suddenly occurred to her that she really didn't know much about

Lukas' past. He knew all about her ex and her earlier life, but he rarely talked about his. The woman had planted enough seeds of doubt to make Annie feel nauseous and weak.

The blonde saw the effect she was having on Annie, so she smirked and continued. "So now he's resorted to seducing squaws?" she said, laughing with no humor. "It doesn't surprise me. He's been through every white girl around." Then she took a step toward Annie threateningly. "What makes you think an ugly little squaw like you could get a man like Lukas? He can have any woman he wants—and he's had a lot of them. Yeah, I decided I wouldn't take his Dom shit anymore. I don't need anyone telling me what to do."

Oh my god, thought Annie, *she seems to know some things about Lukas.*

"Yeah. *I* left *him*. I'm warning you, bitch. Get away from him as fast as you can."

Annie was paralyzed and speechless as the woman turned to walk out the door. Over her shoulder, she called, "Tell him Tracy says hi and she plans to ruin his life the way he ruined hers."

Annie stood without moving. It might have been a minute or an hour, but when she finally turned to the sink and caught a glimpse of herself, she was horrified. Her face reflected shock and grief so profoundly that she barely recognized herself. She didn't know what to do but she *did* know she couldn't face Lukas—or anyone—right now. She had to get away to process everything. She had to get out of there. Though she didn't have her coat, she had her purse and that would have to do. She knew she wasn't thinking straight—it was impossible right now—but she had to be alone.

There was no room for deliberation or common sense as Annie peeked out the restroom door to see an exit sign above a door toward the end of the hallway. She threw open the door to the outside and looked around. She had a general idea of where she was in Green Bay, but it didn't matter. Though it had begun to rain, she just began to walk, and as she did, the nightmare she'd just experienced played on a loop in her head.

Annie knew she shouldn't just accept all Tracy said as true, but the woman clearly knew Lukas, so what was she to think? If it was true—or even if any part of it was true—she would have to leave. The wave of grief that washed over her at that idea was so powerful, she stopped walking, put her hands on her knees and tried to just breathe. Annie had thought she had experienced heartbreak before, but this was agony—the real thing.

As Annie felt it begin to rain harder and turn to sleet, she was dragged back to the reality of the moment. She had to find a place to escape the rapidly deteriorating weather. There were a few hotels in the downtown area and she had credit cards. As she heard a rumble of thunder in the distance, she began to walk faster and seriously consider where she might go. Staying the night would give her the privacy and peace to think through next steps. She walked quickly toward the old Union Hotel whose entrance was warmly lit and welcoming. She tucked into the front door just as the sleet became an icy deluge and Annie pulled herself together to approach the front desk. It was then she realized that she had left Dyani alone and her friend would be worried. She quickly texted her. "I'm okay. Just need some time. Don't worry." Then she turned her phone off, checked in and made her way to the room. Not noticing the charm of the comfortable room, Annie locked the door, threw herself on the bed and cried as if her heart were being carved out with a spoon.

Chapter 19

"I DON'T KNOW," Dyani sobbed as Lukas peppered her with questions. "She said she was going to the restroom, and when she took too long, I went to check on her… there was no sign of her. I should never have let her go alone!" Dyani broke down crying now and Dax pulled her close while giving Lukas a look of warning.

By the time Dax and Lukas arrived at the Black Saddle, Dyani was in a panic. Annie had just disappeared.

"Look, Dyani, this is not your fault in any way. Understand?" said Lukas. He waited for her to nod her head. "If she left the building, she couldn't have gone far, yeah? Can you remember how long ago it was when she headed back there?"

"Not long. Maybe fifteen or twenty minutes now," Dyani said, sniffling.

"It's important that we stay calm and think this through reasonably. You know we'll find her," Lukas said, trying to reassure her—and himself. He put a comforting hand over Dyani's and asked, "Did you notice Annie acting strangely in any way? Did you see her talk with anyone?"

Dyani looked around the crowded bar and said, "There was a guy who looked like he wanted to talk with Annie. He was standing near her, but when she talked to the bartender about reservations, she mentioned that they should be made in her fiancé's name and he left us alone. That's him over there. That big guy," said Dyani, indicating a large man who was in conversation with another woman. Pleased that Annie had used that tactic to discourage a man, Lukas also felt a wave of unwelcome jealousy as he looked over at the man who had spoken to Annie.

Dyani continued to look around and suddenly grabbed Lukas' arm. "Oh, Lukas. There *was* someone else. A woman who was also standing near us. She was tall and blonde—very pretty—but she looked Annie up and down with a nasty stare and I didn't like her right away."

"Is she still here?" asked Lukas, standing to look around the room.

Dyani stood on the rungs of the high bar chair she was sitting on and perused the room. "Yes. I think that's her," she said, indicating the statuesque blonde talking with a couple of men with her back to them.

Just as Lukas looked toward the woman, she also turned her face and they made eye contact. "Goddamn it," said Lukas almost under his breath. Then looking back at Dax and Dyani, he said, "Wait here."

Lukas knew her only too well. The woman was Tracy Sanders, the younger sister of a woman he used to date a couple of years ago. Tracy had been more than an annoyance when he dated her sister Tanya, always showing up where they were and blatantly—and almost obsessively—vying for Lukas' attention. When he finally broke up with Tanya for several reasons—not the least of which was her sister's inappropriate behavior, Tracy had stalked Lukas. She called him incessantly, waited for him outside his home and showed up wherever he was. He had tried talking to her kindly and then more directly, but the obsessive behavior got out of hand and he resorted to a restraining order. She had violated it once and was taken to jail but that seemed to make things worse. Her behavior escalated and she went around telling people slanderous lies about him. She said he had raped a girl and gotten another pregnant and probably plenty of other lies he hadn't heard. Finally, her sister and parents stepped in and took her for some help and that was the last Lukas had known about her. He hadn't seen her in maybe six months—not since he met Annie—and he had hoped she had gone on with her life, but he had a bad feeling about this.

When Tracy turned to see an intense-looking Lukas Mattson coming her way, he noticed a brief look of fear in her eyes that quickly changed to a defensive mask. As he approached, he noticed she took a step back and was unsteady on her feet. She'd been drinking—too much.

Before he could speak, she threw her arms around his neck, saying with a slur, "Lukas Mattson, great to see you."

Lukas put his hands on her waist to physically move her away, but she grabbed his arm and attached herself to his side, spilling her drink on both of them in the process. He decided to play her game then and said, "Tracy, good to see you too. I've been looking for you. Can we find a place to talk that's a little more… private?"

"Sure, Lukas," she said, looking around triumphantly at the people standing nearby. "Let's go to my place."

Lukas didn't say anything but threw some bills on the bar, took her arm and walked her toward the door. While he walked, he grabbed his phone, relieved to see he still had her sister's contact.

"Hold up, Tracy. Can we talk a minute?" he asked, holding her arms tightly to keep her upright and also to see that she didn't run off. "I've been told that you noticed my fiancée at the bar earlier. Is that true?"

Tracy's face went from drunken compliance to anger almost immediately and she yanked herself away from him with surprising strength. "Yeah, I saw that bitch. You can do better than that squaw, Lukas. You're better than that. Come home with me… please. I'll show you a good time," she said as seductively as she could while intoxicated.

Using great effort to diffuse his revulsion and rage, he continued. Maybe she knew where Annie had gone. "Sure. I'll take you home, Tracy," he said with a clenched jaw. "But tell me, did you talk to her?"

Sidling up to Lukas again, Tracy said, "I sure did, honey. I set her straight about you and told her she wasn't good enough for you. And you know what? She knows it too. The little bitch was ready to cry. I think I got rid of her for you."

The picture of Tracy 'attacking' his sweet girl in the restroom had Lukas seeing red. Who knew what lies Tracy told her? Annie must have been devastated and not knowing what to believe or what to do, she ran.

Without another word but still hanging on to Tracy's arm, he made his way to the bouncer. He explained that the woman he was holding was not his friend and was too drunk to drive home. He said that she'd probably make a scene if they called her a cab, but that would still be best.

Lukas said, "Or I can call her family if you can keep an eye on her until they get here," he said, taking a few fifties out of his pocket and handing them to the bouncer. "But I've got to go."

"Yeah. I've been watching her," said the bouncer. "She's in here getting blasted a lot. Today, she's getting out of control. If you'll call her family, I'll take care of her, buddy," said the bouncer who took Tracy's arm and began leading her to a backroom office. About halfway there, she started screaming and swearing like a banshee, but Lukas ignored it as he called his ex-girlfriend Tanya. Luckily, Tanya answered, and briefly, Lukas explained what Tracy had done and encouraged her sister to come and get her, saying she wasn't safe being alone and drunk at the Black Saddle.

"Oh God, Lukas! She's had a relapse. I'm so sorry. We'll come and get her right now. And, Lukas, thank you," said Tanya as Lukas disconnected.

Now that he had an understanding of what might have transpired, he needed to find Annie. He told Dax and Dyani to wait there while he went out to find Annie. He said he'd be calling some police buddies to help him, but he needed them to wait there in case she came back.

"I'll call as soon as I find her," he said. Then he turned to a visibly upset Dyani and said, "Try not to worry. You know I love Annie and I'll find her. I got this."

Chapter 20

THE STORM WAS WINDING down and the rain/sleet had let up some by the time Lukas tore out the back door of the Black Saddle and tried to determine which way Annie might have gone. She would have needed shelter from the storm, so she could be in a store, a hotel or any open building. He figured she would have headed into the downtown area. While he walked, he called his friend Sam, who was a detective for Green Bay PD. He explained the situation to him and asked him if he could track credit card use for Annie Summerhill.

"Isn't that the girl you rescued from that kidnapper last year?" asked Sam.

"Same one. But now, she's my fiancée and I've got to find her, Sam," said Lukas.

"Yeah. I'm on it, Lukas. I'll let you know what I find."

Lukas hated to think about what was going through Annie's head after she heard Tracy's lies, but he knew her state of mind wouldn't be reasonable. She'd feel shocked and betrayed. He wished she'd been able to walk away from Tracy and wait to ask him what it was all about, but he knew that wasn't her style. For all her good qualities, she was also impulsive and had a temper that ran hot. As sympathetic as he was about her feelings, he was also frightened for her safety and angry with her careless choice to take off alone at night in a storm. Lukas decided that after he found her and saw that she was safe and sound, he would let her know that he didn't appreciate the childish way she had handled the situation. He hoped the discussion he had with her bottom would prevent this kind of thoughtless and risky behavior in the future. Had she even considered what could happen to her?

Heedless of the icy rain, Lukas stopped in every open establishment along the main drag—drug stores, bars, restaurants and hotels. He also tried her number every five minutes but all he got was voicemail. He was just coming out of The Marquette House where the front desk clerk had refused to tell him if he saw a woman who fit Annie's description when he got a call back from Sam.

"Yeah. We got some credit card activity at the Union Hotel on Howard. I'm in the area. You want me to meet you there? I may be able to facilitate your search," suggested Sam.

Lukas knew Sam would be able to flash his badge and get the information he needed as well as access to her room.

"That would be a big help, man."

"Be there in five," said Sam helpfully.

Sam was there quickly, and in no time, they'd been able to determine that Annie had indeed checked in and was in room 420. Sam used his badge to obtain a room card and as they made their way to the elevator, he said, "I don't think you need me anymore," and he handed the card to Lukas. "How about I head over to the Black Saddle—see if Tracy left with her sister and let your friends know they can go home?"

Lukas took the key and then shook Sam's hand. "I can't thank you enough, Sam. Really, I owe you."

As Sam made his way down the hall, he heard Lukas gently knock on the door of 420 and say, "Annie. Baby, it's me. Open up."

There was no response so he knocked a little harder. "Annie. Please open the door. I need to see you're okay and we need to talk," he said.

There was a silent pause but then he heard her say, "I need to be alone. Go away."

"I'm not going away," he said more sternly, but then realizing that wouldn't work, he said, "I know you're upset, baby, but if you talk with me, we can work it out."

"But I don't know what to think. She said such terrible things! I want to be alone!" Then he could hear her pitiful crying again. Annie was like a child who was beside herself. Lukas had had enough. He used the card and threw the door open. What he saw broke his heart.

Annie looked devastated. Her face was red and swollen from crying and her wet hair clung to her face and shoulders as her wet clothes did to her body. She was still sniffling and hiccupping and as Lukas stepped into the room, she backed away. He was battling a number of emotions—relief that he found her and she was okay, regret that an old relationship of his had caused her pain, and anger that she had once again acted impulsively, putting herself at risk. But he saw the hurt and confusion in her eyes and moved to wrap his arms around her.

"Baby, baby, you have every reason to be upset, but if you'll listen to me, I can make it better." She remained tense and stiff at first as he sat to hold her on his lap. She was damp and cold so he grabbed a blanket from the bed, wrapped it around her and rocked her gently while he kissed her head, crooning words of comfort. When she felt warmer and seemed calm, Lukas settled her against the pillows on the bed and sat next to her with his arms caging her.

"Are you ready to listen?" he asked firmly, and she nodded her head. "I dated Tracy's sister Tanya a few years ago, for maybe about a year. Tracy's a few years younger than Tanya, and she developed a crush on me that began harmlessly enough but escalated into a kind of obsession. I didn't know this, but Tracy had battled some significant mental and emotional health issues and my presence in her sister's life seem to have triggered a path to breakdown for her," Lukas explained.

He noticed she was listening intently now so he continued. "Things didn't work out between Tanya and me and we broke up. I heard later that Tracy had been sent to a residential treatment facility for help. And that's the last I heard about either of the girls until tonight. I called Tanya to come and get Tracy and she said she had recently suffered a relapse and they'd have to come to a family decision on what do to."

Annie had tears in her eyes and said, "I'm sorry for her."

"I knew you would be, baby, and let me tell you that Tanya is sorry Tracy upset you." He paused then and said, "And so am I. I'm so sorry a past relationship of mine brought this down on you."

Annie nodded and said, "It's not your fault but… but when this woman, this really beautiful woman, started to tell me all these awful things—well, I felt like I had been hit by a truck." Tears coursed down her cheeks when she went on, "I didn't want to believe her, and the things she was saying were mostly outrageous, but some… well, some sounded right."

"What seemed right to you? "he asked, raising her face to look at him.

"Lukas, there was this gorgeous woman saying I wasn't good enough for you and that you had loved her. It seemed like it could be true. We haven't known each other that long and there's a lot I don't know—like about old girlfriends."

Lukas had to control his anger as his hands balled into fists and there was a tick in his jaw. "What else?"

"She said I wasn't the first woman you had asked to marry you. She said it was a line you used. And… and she said you had children—a few children—with other women. Is that true?" she asked as her voice cracked.

Lukas moved to hold her again, saying, "Annie, none of that is true, but it must have been hard to hear. I'm sorry, baby." He took her hands in his and noticed they were like ice. She was still chilled and he thought she was even holding her jaw tight so as not to allow her teeth to chatter.

"Christ, little girl, you're chilled to the bone," he said, rubbing his huge hands up and down her arms. "Let's get you bundled up. We're going home—now, yeah?" he said with authority.

Still feeling raw and unsure, Annie folded her arms over her chest and said, "You know what? There was one more thing she said that proved she knows you."

That stopped Lukas in his tracks. "Oh yeah, what was that?"

"She said you were bossy," Annie said with a challenge.

Lukas looked at his little girl, who seemed to be coming back to the surface. He leaned over her, kissed her on the top of her head and said, "Guilty as charged, baby. Always have been—always will be."

Then he picked her up, still wrapped in a blanket, and though she protested, he carried her out to the truck and buckled her in. He wanted her showered, fed and warm. More talk could wait.

After showering and eating a little something, Lukas crawled into bed with her in a spooning position where she felt so warm and secure that she fell into a deep sleep. She woke up still feeling the warm glow from being held next to Lukas' powerful body all night. When she realized he wasn't there, she felt his absence but she stretched luxuriously, snuggled down into the soft bedding and took the time to process the events of the day before. As she thought about all the poison Tracy had spewed, she realized that she didn't really believe most of it. However, she was still plagued with the question of why Lukas was with her instead of any of the beautiful women who found him attractive. That doubt grabbed at her and made her insecure. Was it that insecurity that had motivated her to run last night? She understood now that her reaction had been impulsive, immature and—Lukas would say—dangerous. She understood that as bad as the situation had been, it wasn't his fault yet she had frightened him, and her good friends, by running off into the dark night in a storm, with no plan. She put her hands in front of her face and shook her head at her foolishness.

"Good morning, baby. Come to breakfast, yeah?" she heard his deep sexy voice say from the doorway.

"I'm not really hungry," she said, not moving to get out of the bed.

He was there in a heartbeat and moved to block her escape, holding her wrists. "Hold up, baby. Listen to me."

Lukas told Annie that Tanya had called to say that Tracy had gone back into residential therapy and to say again to let her know how sorry she was.

Though Annie didn't really want to talk about Lukas' ex, she said sincerely, "That woman must be a trial for her family. I'm glad she's getting help."

"Believe me, baby, she'll never bother you again," he said, patting her legs. "Come on and eat."

Annie's stomach was still a little queasy from the night before, so she said, "I told you—I'm not really hungry." While glad to see some of the old Annie coming back, Lukas wouldn't stand for any defiance—not today. She was immediately sorry she'd been sassy as she recognized the frustrated look on his face.

In one quick move, he lifted her out of the bed, sat down on the edge and stood her between his thighs. When he took her wrists, she tested him by trying to pull away.

"Oh no, baby girl. I think you know why I put you here," Lukas said, lowering his chin.

Annie stopped struggling. Finally, she looked down and said softly, "Yes. I suppose I do."

"Tell me," he said evenly.

She bit her lip and said, "I know that running away when I was upset last night wasn't… well, it was… you'd say risk taking." There was a pause and she said, "I probably should have waited for you and… and asked you about it."

Lukas was relieved that she had come to the right conclusion on her own but knew she would still not like what came next. "That's right, baby. Running out alone, in the dark, in a storm, when no one knew where you were was downright dangerous, yeah?"

Annie nodded sadly.

"And I don't want you ever to do that again."

"But I won't. I won't. I promise," she pleaded.

"I hope not, but I think you knew there'd be consequences, didn't you?" Lukas said, flipping her over one powerful leg, bracing her legs with his other one and pulling down her panties all in one fluid movement.

He wasted no time and began spanking her crisply and then working up the intensity quickly. Lukas wanted her to understand that this wasn't a good girl spanking, but rather a serious one meant to teach a lesson. He knew it had to sting and Annie began begging for all she was worth and he noted that she was more contrite than angry. Maybe she understood that she deserved a punishment and would think things through more carefully next time. Hoping that was the case, he decided that this spanking, while painful, would not be severe. He was mindful of the color of her bottom going from pink to red and also that as she bawled, she seemed repentant. When she went limp over his thigh, he began to let up.

"Running off wildly without talking to me was childish—and not safe. Do you understand that?" He emphasized the question with a smack.

"Yes, Daddy," Annie said, gasping but thinking it seemed an appropriate endearment for the moment.

"I know you were upset, but if you'd waited to talk with me to find out the truth, you wouldn't be in this position now," he said with a spank to her thighs.

Annie squealed and said, "I'm sorry, Daddy."

After a dozen or so more smacks to her bottom and thighs, Lukas was satisfied that she'd learned her lesson and he stopped but kept his paddle-like hand on her backside.

"Ow! Ow!" Annie cried. "Oh, Daddy, I'm so sorry. I see that it was wrong. I won't do it again. Please stop spanking. I'll be good."

Lukas was convinced but didn't let her up right away. He waited until she calmed and noted the deep scarlet color of her bottom along with his handprints on her thighs and knew he had made an impression that he hoped would last. Then he sat her up on his lap and stroked gentle circles on her back while offering her some tissues.

When she leaned into his neck and said, "I'm so sorry, Daddy. I'll never do anything like that again," he was sure he had done the right thing.

"Now, you'll eat some breakfast, yeah?" he asked.

"Okay," she snuffled and reached to pull up her panties.

He stopped her. "You know how I feel about bare bottoms and lessons learned. Take them off."

When she looked up at him pleadingly, he held firm and said, "Now."

So Annie ate her waffles with strawberries while squirming on a sore bare bottom, trying not to pout—as that wasn't allowed, either.

As they both finished, Lukas' heart softened. "Come here, baby," he said, extending his hand so she could stand next to him. He took her hand with one of his and used the other to wrap around her still warm bottom.

"Why don't you go take a shower and I'll clean up here."

She nodded and he watched his little, red-bottomed girl make her way to the bedroom as his cock twitched. *Christ, she had such a hold on him.*

She challenged his control at every turn.

Chapter 21

AFTER HER SHOWER, Annie took extra care brushing her hair out into a gleaming black curtain and wore it loose over a soft, white sweater dress. She left her legs bare and decided it would please him if she didn't wear panties. She put on her favorite black knee length boots and added one small spray of the vanilla scent he seemed to notice and she was ready to face him again. She had to admit that though Lukas had sincerely explained away everything Tracy had thrown at her the night before, the jealous monster that rose up in her when she thought he had been with that tall blonde was hard to tame.

She felt like she needed to win him again—seduce him— and she had to admit she was feeling aroused, not just because she had worked to look sexy for him, but also because she could still feel the sting of his dominance on her bottom. Trying to keep the memory of the spanking out of her head, she made her way out to the great room, to find Lukas standing with his back to her in front of the windows overlooking the deck, drinking a cup of coffee.

His huge form filled the entire window, and for a

moment, she took a private inventory of his extraordinarily masculine body. She appreciated the broad shoulders stretching his shirt across his back, his muscular and perfect backside, and even those strong hands that had not long ago been applying a painful lesson to her bottom. When he turned, put down his coffee and reached for her, she flew to him, already feeling dampness between her legs.

"Christ, Annie. You are the most beautiful woman..." he said as his eyes darkened and he slanted his mouth possessively over hers, taking charge of her mouth. When he reached down to cup her bottom cheeks, she gave a little mewl, so he said, "How's that naughty bottom now? Still a little tender?"

Lifting her chin, he found her blushing. She batted at him as he lifted and carried her to sit on the kitchen counter. Standing in his favorite place, between her legs, he said, "Listen, babe, the dream I had to set up a legal center on Oneida tribal lands is now a dream that we share. And the idea that we not only love each other, but also have the same hopes for the future is remarkable. You're my perfect partner, little girl. We fill in each other's spaces and make a powerful force. I want you at my side every day as we move forward with Solstice Center."

Annie's eyes filled with tears at his tender speech.

"But listen. While it'll be a beautiful thing, difficult situations and even danger will always be a possibility in our work. Whenever you're dealing with the life issues of individuals and families, there's drama and sometimes desperation. Desperation can lead people to do things out of character like taking risks or becoming violent. You see that, right?"

Annie looked up at him, put her hands on his chest, ready to respond, but he continued. "I love you with my life, Annie, and the idea that you could be hurt—or worse—doing this work is difficult for me to think about which is why, now more than ever, I feel the need to put rules in place that will protect you. Do you understand me?" he asked.

She moved her hands from his chest up to his face and said, "I understand, Lukas, that you need to protect me and that you worry about me and that this comes from a place of love. I promise I'll try harder to think about safety before I act. I don't want to be a burden to you."

One of his hands was still covering her entire bottom as he squeezed her cheeks and said, "You can't ever be a burden, baby, and I don't ever want to hear that again, yeah?" When she nodded, he said, "I'm glad to hear that you'll give your actions more thought. Even though I know some situations are beyond your control, I expect you to keep your safety in mind at all times. And if you don't, you'll suffer consequences," he said in his Daddy/Dom voice. When she peeked up at him from under her thick, black lashes, he said, "I'll bare that little bottom and spank or paddle it—every time. You know I'm serious about that, yeah?"

"Yes, Daddy," she said, thinking that he must know the power his words had over her. She began to feel an uncontrollable tingle in her core. Feeling both arousal and trepidation, she lifted her arms around his neck and as she did, her dress rode up so that Lukas could feel her bare bottom.

"No panties, huh? What a naughty girl!" he said, lowering his lips to hers as they willingly parted. He lifted her up so that her legs went around his waist. Lukas made a masculine sound of pleasure and Annie could feel his cock grow.

He carried her into the bedroom and sat down with her straddling his lap as he ordered, "Arms up," and yanked her dress up and off. He grabbed her slender waist and tossed her on the bed. She was completely naked except for her high black boots and the look was so astonishingly erotic, he felt out of control.

Annie saw his look of pure lust and spread her booted legs as far as she could while Lukas crawled over her, saying, "My God, what you do to me, little girl!"

"Please, Daddy, please," she said breathlessly.

"Soon, baby."

He reached into her wet, swollen folds and found her clit waiting for him, and when he moved a calloused finger over it, Annie gave a helpless moan and arched against him. The fading sting in her bottom heightened her desire and as he entered her, he also covered her mouth with his, stifling her cries. Their lovemaking took on an urgent intensity, perhaps because they had finally come to a full understanding of all that their relationship entailed—physical and intellectual attraction, shared devotion to lifetime goals, and the unlikely but priceless bonus of an appreciation of a Daddy Dom/little girl dynamic. The rightness of who they were together and his incredible prowess sent Annie's ecstasy unfurling first as she cried out, "Daddy!" over and over. He could feel her tight sheath spasming around him and he quickly followed, thrusting faster and faster until he went tense, roared her name, and pumped his seed into her in a mind-blowing orgasm. When he was finally sated, he held himself up on his forearms over her and kissed her face and neck. She pulled him down into a slow, deep kiss.

They were both breathless and though it took a long time for their heartrates to return to normal, they stayed wrapped around each other until Annie closed her eyes in bliss and Lukas moved away to get warm cloths to wash her. Then he lay down and began to pull her into a spoon position, but Annie turned in his powerful arms and burrowed her head into his neck, filling all spaces between their bodies. He kissed the top of her head and declared his love for her as she hummed sleepily in satisfaction.

Chapter 22

THERE WERE JUST two days until their courthouse nuptials were to take place and both Lukas and Annie were very busy. He continued meetings with stakeholders and board members as plans came together for the legal center. She accompanied him sometimes, especially when there was anything about the secure shelter for women and children being discussed. The idea was encouraged at every turn, but finding the funding to do all they hoped would be an additional challenge. Lukas' wealth allowed him to decline a salary of any kind and he also had some assets he could liquidate, including his family homestead in Brussels, to help things get going.

"No, Lukas. I don't want you to give up your childhood home to fund Solstice Center. Can't we just slow down—do one thing at a time as we set up long range fundraising?" Annie asked as they ate breakfast together on Thursday morning.

"Maybe," said Lukas, "but the programs would be so much more effective if they could be launched at the same time. I'm going to sit down with my accountant early next week to work out a few different routes we could take. Dax has offered some help, but I don't know exactly what he's thinking. I guess I'll have to pin him down."

When Annie's brow furrowed, Lukas could see she was anxious.

"Hey, baby. There's no need to worry. Everything will work out," he said, cradling one of her cheeks with his great hand. "All you need to worry about for the next day is marrying me, yeah?"

She looked up at him with love and said dreamily, "Yeah, though I still can't believe you want to marry me."

In a flash, Lukas had her upended and was delivering sharp smacks to her bottom. "What did I tell you about talking like that? I won't have it, Annie. Understand?"

"Ow! Ow! Yes, Lukas. I understand. Please stop!" she cried as tears pooled in her eyes.

He pulled her into his arms then and said, "You're mine, Annie Summerhill, and tomorrow, it will be legally real. You'll be Annie Mattson." Rubbing his hands gently up and down her back, he said, "You know, baby, that you agreed to be my wife, has made me happier than I ever thought possible. I love you. Don't ever think I don't. Promise me."

"I promise, Lukas," she said, looking over her shoulder at him with a seductive smile.

He picked her up, stood her between his legs and gave her one swat. "Don't think to tempt me today, baby. We haven't got time; there's lots to do."

She immediately moved one hand to her offended bottom, put her other one up to his chest and pouted.

"No pouting, either," he said.

"Maybe you could kiss my pout away?" Annie peeped, biting her full lower lip and batting her eyelashes.

"Christ, you're killing me, baby," he said as he lowered his mouth to her parting lips and kissed her with blatant possession. When she moaned into his mouth, he knew he was gone and he yanked her yoga pants down and pulled them off as he lifted her to straddle his lap. Then he grabbed her bottom cheeks to squeeze them and let his fingers move to her folds. "God, I love how you're always ready for me, little girl," he said into her ear as he reached to unzip his jeans and free his already rock-hard cock.

He quickly positioned himself and entered her with one powerful thrust that had her gasping. As always, she needed a few moments to adjust to his size, but then she arched her back as euphoria quickly claimed her, and she began to ride him. She had never taken charge like that before and was unsure of his reaction. She needn't have worried.

"Goddamnit, Annie! I love the way you move. Keep going, baby," he said as she allowed his cock to slip to her opening and then drill back up into her. He took over then— as she knew he would— and grabbed her hips so hard, she was sure she would have bruises. As he pumped in and out, he reached one hand back to find her clit. When he stroked it with a rough finger while still thrusting into her, she felt an orgasm careening toward completion as she threw her head back and screamed his name. At that very moment, he wrapped his arms around her tightly and stilled within her as she felt his release fill her. She continued to spasm around him.

"Christ, Annie. I goddamn love you!"" he said as she held his head between her breasts.

They held on while their breathing calmed, and as they floated back to reality, Lukas stood with her and took her to the bathroom to gently clean them up.

When he finished, Annie took his face in her hands and said with a mischievous smile, "Oh, Lukas, I'm so glad you could fit me into your busy schedule today. Thank you, kind sir."

Lukas threw his head back and laughed hard at that, but as he laughed, he picked her up, sat down on the bed and pulled her still bare bottom over his lap.

"Lukas, no! Stop! I don't deserve a spanking!" she squealed.

"Oh no? Well, let's see. First, I told you not to tempt me, but you did. Then you tried to take charge in the bedroom. I know we've talked about the consequences of that. Who's in charge, baby?" he said as she squirmed on his lap trying to escape.

"You are, Daddy. You're in charge. I'm sorry. I don't want a spanking," she pleaded.

"So let's see, you defied me twice and then got sassy," he said. "Don't you think you deserve a spanking?"

When she said nothing but went quiet in his arms, he lightly pinched one cheek, prompting her to say, "Maybe. Maybe I do deserve a-a spanking—a little one.

His expression softened at that and he lifted her up off his lap, patted her bottom and said, "I don't know what I'm going to do with you, but for now, get dressed so we can get going, yeah?"

Left alone in the bedroom, Annie had a chance to think her own thoughts about the fact that tomorrow, she would marry her love. She was thrilled that he loved her, but a courthouse wedding seemed unromantic and anticlimactic. They would just wake up to a regular Friday. They'd get dressed up and drive to the courthouse and that would be that—nothing special—no traditions. The idea of foregoing all those important memories saddened her. She knew Dyani's marriage and wedding reception had been separate, just like theirs would be. How had she done it? How had she felt? She knew Lukas would be waiting for her, but she had to call her friend—now!

Dyani understood Annie's feelings right away, and as they talked, Dyani suggested that maybe Annie would like to spend the night at their house so the bride and groom would be traditionally apart. The young women could get ready together and it would fun. Dax and Dyani would accompany her to the courthouse where she could make a memorable entrance at the beginning of the ceremony.

Annie loved the idea and agreed before talking with Lukas. She thanked her friend, grabbed her overnight bag and began packing everything she would need at Dyani's. And that's what Lukas saw her doing when he came to get her.

She didn't see him in the doorway at first as she rushed around trying to make sure she had everything.

"You're leaving me?" he asked evenly, leaning on the doorframe with his hands in his pockets.

Surprised, she looked up, suddenly realizing she hadn't talked to him about spending the night away but had rather just decided herself. He was sure not to like that.

"Oh," she said with a nervous laugh. "Of course not!"

He had a confused look on his face when he looked from Annie to the overnight bag and back.

"Oh yes—this," she said as she went to him, put her hands on his broad chest and looked up at him imploringly. "You know, I was thinking. It's bad luck for the groom to see the bride before the ceremony so I thought—well, Dyani and I thought—maybe I should stay with them tonight so we—"

"Absolutely not!" Lukas thundered. The look on his face made Annie back up a few steps.

"But, Lukas, it's bad luck," she said, knowing how weak that sounded.

"I said no!" said Lukas, sounding not quite as angry but certainly resolute.

Annie did something then that she rarely did. She burst into tears and covered her face with her hands. It was a genuine reaction, but it made her feel out of control.

Lukas was unprepared for this unusual reaction from her and he didn't like it. "Annie baby," he said, reaching for her to hold her in his arms. "I'm sorry I yelled at you. Let's talk about this. Come on."

He picked her up and carried her to the great room, where he sat in his leather chair and drew her onto his lap. He grabbed some tissues to mop up her face. Her crying had now been reduced to sniffles and hiccups.

"Better?" he asked. When she nodded, he said gently, "Good. Why don't you tell me what you're thinking?"

When she looked up at him, she saw the concerned face of the man she loved and she knew she could tell him what was important to her. She took a deep breath and moved on his lap to face him.

With her hands once again on his chest, she said, "I know you've promised me a real wedding and reception in the future, and I love you for that, but tomorrow, is more than… more than just a legal process. We'll be joined as husband and wife forever, beginning tomorrow. It's a life changing day and I think it would be so lovely if we could make it a little special. It we're apart for just tonight, I'll be able to open that courtroom door tomorrow and there you'll be, waiting for me. And there I'll be, wanting so badly for you to be my husband. It's a memory I want to make with you. Won't you please allow it?" She said all of this at once, speaking fast, but now stopped on a sob. "Please, Daddy. Please let me stay with Dyani tonight."

Lukas was shocked but also deeply touched by Annie's sweet plea. The idea would never have entered his mind, but clearly, it meant a great deal to his little girl. He hated the idea of not having her in his bed tonight, but in the grand scheme of things, this seemed like a small thing to do for her.

"If it's so important to you, I'll agree. I'll miss you, though," he said, grabbing her hands and pulling her to him to share a meaningful kiss.

Finally, he broke away to hold her and as he did, she whispered, "Thank you, Daddy. I love you."

Chapter 23

AS THE GIRLS sat together on the king-sized bed sharing a bottle of sweet white wine, Dyani smiled and said, "You seem so happy now, Annie. I mean, remember how long it took you to let Lukas in and then how hard it was for you to deal with... with his dominance?"

"I do. I put up so many barriers. I'm so lucky he kept pursuing me... putting up with me," she said wistfully, finishing her glass of wine. "I love him with all that I am, Dyani. I hope I can make him happy."

"You already do that, except when you take risks," Dyani said, smiling.

"Oh, I don't know. I think he's happy spanking me too," she said as they both dissolved into giggles.

Dax appeared in the doorway then, saying, "It's getting late and it sounds like you've both had plenty of wine. Time for you two to get some sleep."

Annie yawned tellingly, thanked her hosts and went to bed, but not to sleep. As she lay there, wide awake, she had second thoughts about the wisdom of spending the night away from Lukas. In the last few weeks, they had been together day and night. She was used to feeling his presence near her and the easy way he would casually touch her and kiss her during the day and the way he held her—and made love to her—each night. Tonight, her heart ached for missing him. But it would be that much sweeter when she saw him tomorrow, and she couldn't wait. Thoughts of Lukas finally stopped spinning through her mind and she fitfully slept.

The girls spent the next morning talking, giggling and getting ready. They had dressed in fluffy white robes after their showers and Dyani was so excited, she could barely contain herself. When Dax called them to lunch, Dyani balked at the interruption.

"Oh, Dax, we don't want to eat right now. I'm just starting on Annie's hair. Can you just cover the sandwiches and we'll eat later?" she said, not even pausing from brushing Annie's thick tresses.

Dax was suddenly in the doorway—filling the doorway, actually—and his face was stern.

"You two need to eat—now," he said in a voice that Dyani would have taken seriously on any other day, but on this day, she was distracted and excited. When she didn't respond, Dax took a step into the room.

"Come here," he ordered so harshly that both girls froze. She hesitated momentarily, but then Dyani stomped over to Dax with an attitude, ignoring his escalating annoyance at her behavior. As she stood in front of him, he took her arm and said, "You need to come eat something now. You'll still have a couple of hours to get ready."

When Dyani stamped her foot like a child and began to argue further, Annie was shocked and put her hand up to her mouth wondering if she should interfere. But before she could speak, Dax began to pull her from the room. He briefly glanced at Annie and said, "Excuse us please."

Dyani understood she had gone too far and didn't struggle as Dax led her out of the room. He took her into the next bedroom and Annie could hear everything.

Within seconds, she heard Dyani begin pleading with him not to spank her, but then she heard the distinct sounds of a hand slapping a bare bottom and Dyani promising to be good. He spanked about twenty times until Dyani was sobbing.

"You know that when you act like a child, you'll get treated like one." *Smack. Smack. Smack.* "You've let your excitement about today get out of control." *Smack. Smack. Smack.* "Are you ready to settle down?" *Smack. Smack. Smack.*

"Yes, Daddy, I'm sorry. Please stop," Dyani frantically cried.

And then it was quiet. Annie let out a breath she hadn't known she was holding and put her hands up to her cheeks to cool them. Annie knew about the Daddy/little girl dynamic that was part of their relationship—in fact, she understood it. But their relationship seemed a bit more pronounced than hers with Lukas. Dax was more strict and Dyani more of a little girl than Annie. She knew it worked for them and that she, too, was heading into a life with a dominant man who sometimes spanked and wanted to be called Daddy. She was embarrassed for her friend and, she had to admit, missing Lukas even more. Annie was also unsure of what to do next.

She needn't have worried. It was just a minute or two before Dyani rushed back to Annie with Dax standing behind her in the doorway.

"Oh, Annie, I'm so sorry I embarrassed you today, of all days. I'm just so excited for you, I can barely stand it. Please forgive me!" she said, throwing her arms around her as more tears escaped her eyes.

Annie patted her back and said, "There's nothing to forgive. You're such a good friend." And then looking up to Dax but still speaking to Dynai, she said, "Let's get some lunch, and then I can work on your hair too." Dax winked at Annie and they enjoyed some white chicken chili and crusty bread. Though Dyani squirmed uncomfortably in her chair, her cheerful manner had returned.

They spent the next few hours getting ready. This worked out for Dax, as he had arranged a few surprises for the newlyweds and had to make some last minute calls. Finally, by about two o'clock, they were headed to the Brown County Courthouse.

It was three thirty on a Friday afternoon when courthouse staff would be ready to leave for the weekend, but everyone, from the security guards, to the receptionist, to the clerk of courts, seemed happy to be part of a marriage ceremony. Annie and Dyani were shown to an anteroom off the courtroom where they could do a final freshen-up while the men waited with the judge in front of the bench. Several Brown County employees had asked to be present as witnesses and Lukas was sure Annie would like that. It seemed much more like a real wedding to have some people there.

The courthouse—like many buildings in Green Bay—was historic, and this particular courtroom had beautiful woodwork everywhere as well as an ornately painted ceiling, a brilliant chandelier and twelve-foot windows.

The last rays of autumn sun were streaming in those windows, giving the room a nostalgic glow. As the grandfather clock in the room signified it was time, Annie suddenly heard the sweet strains of a string quartet coming from the courtroom. Her hand flew to her mouth as she said, "What? How?"

Dyani squeezed Annie's hand and said, "This day is so important, and Dax and I wanted to make it as special as it could be. The quartet was Dax's idea. I know you will have a full-blown wedding later but, well, we wanted to make it memorable for you both." Then she kissed Annie's cheek and said," You look so beautiful, Annie. I'm so happy for you." The girls hugged one more time and Dyani said, "Now, I'll open the door and walk down to meet them. Wait until I'm there, and stand in the doorway until you know Lukas sees you. Then come down the aisle to meet him. It's all going to be lovely, Annie."

As Dyani went ahead, Annie peeked around the door and was able to look at Lukas unobserved for a moment. Her breath hitched as she was reminded of his size that always made her feel safe and his impossible good looks which aroused her every time. He truly took her breath away. His custom-tailored suit fit perfectly, enhancing his muscular form. A ray of sun caught his hair so that it shone red/gold. Annie actually pinched herself, to make sure this wasn't a dream and that the kind, intelligent, loving—and more than hot— Viking waiting for her was really going to be her husband.

Then she came out to stand in the middle of the double doors and, taking Dyani's advice, waited until she knew he saw her. She knew it when his face broke out into a genuine and loving smile and she could see his dimples under his trimmed beard. As Annie stood there, she didn't realize that a beam of sunlight from a large anteroom window created a backlight to her form that made her appear ethereal to those looking her way. Dyani put her hand up to her mouth in wonder and Lukas' face went from smiling to awestruck. When their eyes met, she was briefly paralyzed by the connection and it wasn't until he held out his hand to her that she could move. He watched in a daze as she walked down the room-length aisle toward his extended hand. He took in the bared shoulders that peeked out from underneath her gleaming black hair. On her head, was a crown of small yellow coneflowers which matched the simple bouquet she carried. The soft, gray-green dress flattered her curves as the color complimented her golden skin tone. Her gray suede boots came up past her knees, revealing just a patch of thigh between dress and boot. Lukas found her so beautiful, his heart hurt.

She took his hand and he drew her close, their eyes still locked.

The judge cleared his throat, but when neither Annie or Lukas gave him their attention, he began. They repeated their vows as if there were no one else in the room, and when they were pronounced man and wife, Lukas reached for her, slanted his mouth over hers and kissed her so long and so passionately that everyone was silent. Then those gathered broke out into spontaneous applause and the spell was broken. The clerk had the license for them to sign, witnesses congratulated them, and Dyani did her best to control her tears of happiness.

Outside, at the top of the long entrance stairway, Dyani asked them to stop for a picture. As they wrapped their arms around each other, Lukas put his lips to her ear and asked, "How do you feel, my beautiful little girl?"

"Like I must be dreaming, Daddy," she whispered, standing on tiptoes to capture his lips in a kiss that had her melting.

Lukas' reluctant little girl was finally his forever.

The day had been magical, but the big surprises came as they all celebrated later together at the White Gull Inn. Dax had arranged for a limo to drive them to Fish Creek about an hour up the shore in Door County. And while they rode together, Dax revealed plans that would make it possible for Lukas' plan for a resource center to explode into reality in the near future.

As the limo made its way out of Green Bay and entered Door County, the friends drank champagne and relived the happy afternoon. But soon, Dax found that Dyani could hardly contain herself. She knew that Dax had a spectacular gift for the newlyweds and she couldn't wait. She tugged at his sleeve and wriggled like an excited puppy.

"Tell them," she whispered excitedly. "Tell them the best part."

Dax raised an eyebrow at Dyani and said, "Settle, little girl, before you ruin it by getting in trouble." Dyani immediately stilled as Dax said, "You both know that Dyani and I are so proud of your plans to bring otherwise inaccessible services to Oneida families. But we're more than proud. We want you to know that we completely support your effort and that we want to be part of it," he said, drawing Dyani to his side. "Your plans are ambitious, the Solstice Center for legal and resource help, two secure family shelters, and a new and fully-equipped community center. My understanding is that your funding will come—over time—from tribal and private grants and that you," he said, looking at Lukas, "wish to sell your family homestead in order to jump start construction. Have I got that all right?"

Annie couldn't help but speak up but didn't look at Lukas when she said, "I really don't want Lukas to sell the farm in Brussels. I think we could just go slower and eventually get the funding or a loan for some of the projects." She ventured a peek up at him then and saw a disapproving look.

"We've already had this discussion, Annie, and the subject is closed. Understand?"

Annie lowered her eyes, blushed and nodded.

There was an uncomfortable moment of silence before Dax said, "Well, we've been thinking about this— a lot—and we've decided that the two of us would like to ask to be partners in this venture. You two have the combined extraordinary skills to make this all happen, and your heartfelt commitment is apparent. We want you to know that we, too, are prepared to do our part to make it happen," Dax said.

"What are you saying, Dax?" asked Lukas.

"You've shown me all the details and I understand the financial commitment. If you'll allow us, we'd like to fully fund the Solstice Center project," Dax announced.

Then an excited Dyani jumped in, "Dax will fund it all! The buildings, the staff and the programming. Everything! You don't have to worry or wait!"

Wide eyed, with their mouths open, Lukas and Annie were speechless.

"What do you think?" asked Dax, looking at Lukas.

Before he could speak, Annie began to sob, saying, "This is the most generous gift. I really can't believe it!" Then she turned to her new husband. "Lukas?"

Lukas found his voice, though it was filled with emotion, and he pulled the now sobbing Annie close to his side. "I know you to be a thoughtful, gracious and generous man, Dax, but this offer is something I would never have dreamed of. I'm stunned," Lukas said sincerely.

"You and Annie have a dream, and Dyani and I want to make that dream become a reality now—and completely," he said. But before Lukas could answer, Dax said, "I want you to know that I see our role as a foundational funder and a business consultant, should you need one. We have no intention of micromanaging anything. This is your baby, and there are no two people more well-suited. Please say you will accept."

Lukas looked at Annie and she could see there were tears in his eyes as he said, "We do, with deep gratitude."

Epilogue

"I really don't have the words to thank you, Annie. You saved us and helped us begin a new life. I'll never forget you," said Dakota Cornelius. Dakota had come to Light and Day— the women and children's shelter that was part of the Solstice Center project created by Annie and Lukas— a few months ago. With help from Annie and other professionals at the shelter, Dakota was well on her way to healing and was heading up to Minneapolis to live with a cousin and attend a culinary school. Annie had procured tuition and child care grants and provided an interest free loan for a dependable car. Lukas had provided pro bono work to obtain a divorce for Dakota, and though her ex was serving time, Lukas had made sure he received meaningful treatment for his addiction.

It was a beautiful day. In fact, it was the summer solstice —the longest day of the year—as Annie walked out to the porch with Dakota and her daughter Dani to say goodbye. The sky was that brilliant blue that was unique to June and they were greeted with the gentle scent of honeysuckle. They said their goodbyes and Annie waved from the porch with tears in her eyes as the little family drove away.

Annie's heart was full as she took a moment to sit on the sun-drenched porch and reflect on the progress of the dream she shared with Lukas to provide a legal and resource center as well as a secure shelter that was available to Oneida families.

As it turned out, the magnitude of needs for individual and families who lived on tribal lands had been underestimated. There had been such a backlog from years of neglect that many fell into the desperate and urgent category. Lukas' plate was full of legal work, involving everything from mediation between neighbors, work related conflict and divorce, all the way to the human trafficking and attempted homicide. Early on, they also saw a need for addiction and mental health treatment and would address that soon. Recognizing the volume of work was unsustainable, Dax provided funding to hire two more lawyers and two paralegals. Lukas was still busy, but it was manageable.

Annie helped to oversee the secure shelter that was now located in the house she had rented. As it was a twenty-four-hour facility, there was a staff of twelve that included counselors, social workers, family advocates and security personnel. Annie's main focus, though, was on connecting shelter guests as well as Lukas' clients with resources available in the community, such as energy services, financial counseling, job placement, medical care and affordable housing. It was a big job and Lukas watched carefully that she did not take on too much. He had insisted that she hire two assistants after the first two weeks they were open.

There were glitches and issues to work out, but in general, the initial rollout of Solstice Center was a huge success and it didn't take long for other tribal entities in and outside of the state to contact them for advice on how to duplicate their model.

And this strong start happened even before much of the brick and mortar infrastructure was in place. Other than the one shelter, which was a refurbished house, all other work was done out of older buildings that already existed and were inconvenient and crowded. But progress on other structures was coming along—most importantly, on the main building which would house several resource offices, a diaper bank, a food pantry and a large community space. That building would be the centerpiece for the Solstice Center project. Annie sighed with happy satisfaction when she thought about all that had been accomplished.

Her thoughts were interrupted when she heard the ringtone her phone reserved for Lukas.

"Hi, babe, what are you doing?" he asked.

Annie explained that she had just said good bye to Dakota and Dani and was sitting on the porch counting her blessings. She heard him chuckle and say, "Listen. Can you get a couple of staff to cover for you so I can pick you up in about an hour? They're going to lift the skylight onto the main building today and I thought you'd want to see it. Dax and Dyani are coming down too."

"Oh, I'm so excited! I'll be ready to go when Issi gets back form picking up supplies," she said happily.

There was a pause then before Lukas said, "You're not there alone, are you, little girl?"

With Dakota and Dani gone, there was only one family left at the shelter now, so she had thought it would be okay to send Issi on an errand. She knew she had agreed with Lukas never to be alone at the shelter, but everything had been going so smoothly and it was the middle of the day—she was sure she would be safe. But Lukas wouldn't see it that way. His strong opinion was that Annie had been in too many dangerous situations and the risks of an angry ex showing up at the shelter were just too high for her to be alone—ever. There were security guards protecting the shelter at night, but during the day, they relied on the digital security system and common sense. Annie already regretted sending Issi away but she knew she couldn't lie to Lukas. After a long pause, she told him the truth—she was there alone.

"I don't know what you were thinking, Annie. I've had this discussion with your bottom a number of times now, but I see that I haven't made an impression. That's going to change tonight," he said angrily. "Now I'm going to send Jackson up from the farm to stay there with you until I get there from Green Bay. Understand?" he said.

"Okay," she said contritely. "Lukas, I'm sorry—"

"Not as sorry as you will be later. Get inside and make sure security is set and wait for me." Lukas' stern voice usually caused a tingle inside her, but this time, she knew she had disappointed him and the spanking she would get would not be of the 'good-girl' variety.

She sighed, went inside and tried to freshen up before her angry husband arrived.

But an hour later, it wasn't her husband who pulled up in front of the shelter—it was Dax and Dyani. Lukas had asked that they pick her up on the way as he was supervising the installation. Relieved to postpone "talking" with Lukas about her transgression, she rode with her friends to the construction site about two miles from the shelter.

Annie had seen the architectural drawings for Solstice Center and had visited the site as construction progressed over the last six months. Dax had found a well-known architect from California to design a structure that would use the sun's energy for most of the heating and cooling needs of the building. Solar panels covering most of the roof of the structure would blend perfectly with the glass and steel exterior walls. Eventually, strategic landscaping would soften the lines of the building, helping it fit in to its natural setting.

After talking with Lukas and Annie, the designer understood the significance of the sun as a symbol representing a pathway of light to those who came to use the Solstice Center for help and guidance. Annie was thrilled when the final design included a center court atrium with a dramatic twenty-foot round, raised skylight that would sit thirty feet above the ground level and allow abundant sunlight to flood the center of the building. The steel beams cast artful shadow designs on the walls and floor of what would be an impressive common area. That area would be used for various gatherings and ceremonies, and it was the placement of the skylight that they had come to witness.

The site for the Solstice Center had been chosen so that it would sit on a lot that was naturally higher than the land around it and had a dense woods at its back. As Dax drove up the gentle incline to the building site, Annie realized that though she had been a frequent observer of the building progress, nothing had prepared her for the sight in front of her now. She couldn't help but gasp with wonder.

Lukas was there waiting as Annie burst out of the truck and ran to him.

"Oh, Lukas, this is so incredible!" she said as he pulled her into his side and they watched the work together.

There were two huge cranes, each holding one half of the skylight structure. One crane had positioned its giant piece above the roof. Two teams of men were positioned on the roof to help guide the piece into place and hold it there while the other half was placed. The dangerous process was a once-in-a-lifetime sight and those watching were struck silent.

When half the skylight was in place, more workers moved to grab the second piece. Moving with such speed and efficiency that the operation looked choreographed, the men soon had the massive skylight in place and secured.

The effect was incredible. The glass dome seemed to burst upward out of the strong new structure, reaching toward the light and power of the sun. The glass and steel beamed skylight reflected the remarkably blue June sky. It was an awesome sight to behold and the four friends were in awe.

As the workers made their way down from the roof, the foreman, carrying four hard hats, walked toward the group. They donned the hard hats and after admiring the work and congratulating the crew, the foreman led them inside. As they passed through the foyer, they were treated to their first sight of the breathtaking light and shadow show that bathed the entire interior of the atrium. The sun's light streamed through the top of the skylight, but the expansive pattern created by the diamond-shaped panes and narrow steel bars was stunning. And that glorious pattern would move with the sun throughout the day, making it seem almost alive and in tune with the natural world around it. The space seemed almost sacred.

Annie held her hand out to Dyani as they came together under the skylight, entwining their arms behind each other's backs. As the sun and shadows played against their upturned faces, they made an iconic picture of a bright future for their Oneida people. Both men were nearly moved to tears at the sight.

Dax took it all in but then went to Dyani and said, "It's time for us to get going, baby. We'll come back down in a few days."

Dyani nodded, gave Annie a hug and walked out with her husband, leaving Annie and Lukas alone. Annie reached up to put her arms around Lukas' neck and, looking up, said, "This. This is all because of you. I don't know what I did to deserve a man as wonderful as you. You've made me so happy!"

"We're a team, baby. And all of this; it's a miracle," he said, using his arms to indicate the entirety of the building—the entirety of the concept.

He kissed her then, but when she met his tender kiss with a passionate one of her own, he lifted her so that her legs went naturally around his waist. He walked with her to the nearest wall, backing her up against it, holding her in place. He placed a trail of kisses from her chin and neck across her collarbone, and she whimpered. But when she felt him get hard against her and her breathing began to come in pants, she whispered frantically, "Oh, Lukas, we have to stop. The workmen are still here."

He knew she was right, so he forced himself to pull away, but before he set her down, she put her forehead against his and said, "I love you, Lukas Mattson. I love everything about you!"

He set her down then and raised her chin with his fingers. "Everything? You love *everything* about me?" he said, moving one hand down to cover her bottom.

Instantly, she understood what he meant and she backed away and positioned her splayed hands behind herself protectively. "Well, maybe not *everything*," she said quietly.

He chuckled then and asked, "But you're my little girl, yeah?"

"I guess so," she said, looking up at him with trepidation.

"If you have to 'guess', then you need a reminder that you'll always be my little girl—a reluctant little girl, but nonetheless mine. I'm sure you remember what happens to little girls who don't follow the rules about never being alone," he said in the deep, stern voice that had her panties growing damp. "You're getting a spanking when we get home. Understand?"

"Yes, Daddy," she said as she realized that she *did* understand—everything.

Annie wasn't surprised that Lukas actually used a paddle to make his point when they got home. It was the worst spanking she'd ever received and it *did* make a memorable impression.

When he turned her around to hold her on his lap—bottom still stinging and bare—he asked, "Did my naughty girl learn her lesson?"

Annie nodded and said, "Yes, Daddy." And just those shared words sent a jolt of arousal through her as she turned her face into his neck and put one arm up to his shoulder.

Annie no longer suffered over or even wondered at the strange dichotomy between her need to demonstrate independence and her desire to submit to the dominance of her beautiful Viking. They were two parts of her psyche that seemed to fit together like the puzzle they were. She had also learned not to overthink the fact that the pain of a spanking often morphed into arousal so strong that she was more than wet and ready for Lukas after he had turned her bottom bright red. She thanked the powers that be that Lukas had been patient with her as her reluctance to accept the reality of their relationship went on for months.

As he lifted her now to sit straddling him, his large hands grasping her still-hot bottom, he said in his deep, raspy voice, "Ready for me, baby?"

"Yes, Daddy," she said with a moan and knew she would always be his little girl.

Hannah Kane

Hannah Kane dove right into writing with her first romance series, *Love Signs*. The first book, *Signs of Love* was released in August 2021 with others - *Signs of Courage* and *Signs of Hope* - following later in the year.

Hannah believes the gift of story came from her mother and was so deeply instilled that she became a children's librarian and professional storyteller.

Hannah now spends her days working part time in a crisis center, enjoying family and friends in the comfort of the lakeside neighborhood where she grew up, and of course, happily writing romance.

Blushing Books

Blushing Books is one of the oldest eBook publishers on the web. We've been running websites that publish spanking and BDSM related romance and erotica since 1999, and we have been selling eBooks since 2003. We hope you'll check out our hundreds of offerings at http://www.blushingbooks.com.

Blushing Books Newsletter

Please join the Blushing Books newsletter
to receive updates & special promotional offers.
You can also join by using your mobile phone:
Just text **BLUSHING** to 22828.